I0822516

To Felix, with the best wishes, from Flora.

January 1st 1880.

LOUISA M. ALCOTT'S FAMOUS BOOKS

"Sing, Tessa; sing!" cried Tommo, twanging away with all his might. — PAGE 47.

AUNT JO'S SCRAP-BAG: Containing "My Boys," "Shawl-Straps," "Cupid and Chow-Chow," "My Girls." 4 vols. Price of each, $1.00.

ROBERTS BROTHERS, PUBLISHERS, *Boston*

H. H.'S YOUNG FOLKS' BOOK.

BITS OF TALK,

IN VERSE AND PROSE,

FOR YOUNG FOLKS.

BY H. H.,

AUTHOR OF "BITS OF TALK ABOUT HOME MATTERS," "BITS OF TRAVEL," "VERSES."

"—— in all the lands
No such morning-glory." — PAGE 133.

PRICE $1.00.

ROBERTS BROTHERS, PUBLISHERS,
Boston.

" Promise that I may make the flowers you wear on your wedding-day," whispered Lizzie, kissing the kind hand held out to help her rise. — PAGE 85.

THE AUTOBIOGRAPHY OF AN OMNIBUS. — *Page* 187.

AUNT JO'S SCRAP-BAG.

MY GIRLS, ETC.

BY LOUISA M. ALCOTT,

AUTHOR OF "LITTLE WOMEN," "AN OLD-FASHIONED GIRL," "LITTLE MEN,"
"HOSPITAL SKETCHES," "EIGHT COUSINS," ETC.

BOSTON:
ROBERTS BROTHERS.
1878.

Cambridge:
Press of John Wilson & Son.

CONTENTS.

AUNT JO'S SCRAP-BAG.

I.

MY GIRLS.

ONCE upon a time I wrote a little account of some of the agreeable boys I had known, whereupon the damsels reproached me with partiality, and begged me to write about them. I owned the soft impeachment, and promised that I would not forget them if I could find any thing worth recording.

That was six years ago, and since then I have been studying girls whenever I had an opportunity, and have been both pleased and surprised to see how much they are doing for themselves now that their day has come.

Poor girls always had my sympathy and respect, for necessity soon makes brave women of them if they have any strength or talent in them; but the well-to-do girls usually seemed to me like pretty butterflies, leading easy, aimless lives when the world was full of work which ought to be done.

Making a call in New York, I got a little lesson, which caused me to change my opinion, and further investigation proved that the rising generation was wide awake, and bound to use the new freedom well. Several young girls, handsomely dressed, were in the room, and I thought, of course, that they belonged to the butterfly species; but on asking one of them what she was about now school was over, I was much amazed to hear her reply, "I am reading law with my uncle." Another said, "I am studying medicine;" a third, "I devote myself to music," and the fourth was giving time, money, and heart to some of the best charities of the great city.

So my pretty butterflies proved to be industrious bees, making real honey, and I shook hands with sincere respect, though they did wear jaunty hats; my good opinion being much increased by the fact that not one was silly enough to ask for an autograph.

Since then I have talked with many girls, finding nearly all intent on some noble end, and as some of them have already won the battle, it may be cheering to those still in the thick of the fight, or just putting on their armor, to hear how these sisters prospered in their different ways.

Several of them are girls no longer; but as they are still unmarried, I like to call them by their old name, because they are so young at heart, and have so beautifully fulfilled the promise of their youth, not only by doing, but being excellent and admirable women.

A is one in whom I take especial pride. Well-born, pretty, and bright, she, after a year or two of society, felt the need of something more satisfactory, and, following her taste, decided to study medicine. Fortunately she had a father who did not think marriage the only thing a woman was created for, but was ready to help his daughter in the work she had chosen, merely desiring her to study as faithfully and thoroughly as a man, if she undertook the profession that she might be an honor to it. A *was* in earnest, and studied four years, visiting the hospitals of London, Paris, and Prussia; being able to command private lessons when the doors of public institutions were shut in her face because she was a woman. More study and work at home, and then she had the right to accept the post of resident physician in a hospital for women. Here she was so

AUNT JO'S SCRAP-BAG.

MY GIRLS, ETC.

BY LOUISA M. ALCOTT,

AUTHOR OF "LITTLE WOMEN," "AN OLD-FASHIONED GIRL," "LITTLE MEN,"
"HOSPITAL SKETCHES," "EIGHT COUSINS," ETC.

BOSTON:
ROBERTS BROTHERS.
1878.

every day but the seventh was spent in the National Gallery, copying Turner's pictures in oil and water colors. So busy, so happy, so wrapt up in delightsome work, that food and sleep seemed impertinencies, friends were forgotten, pleasuring had no charms, society no claims, and life was one joyful progress from the blue Giudecca to the golden Sol de Venezia, or the red glow of the old Temeraire. "Van Tromp entering the mouth of the Texel" was more interesting to her than any political event transpiring in the world without; ancient Rome eclipsed modern London, and the roar of a great city could not disturb the "Datur Hora Quieti" which softly grew into beauty under her happy brush.

A spring-tide trip to Stratford, Warwick, and Kenilworth was the only holiday she allowed herself; and even this was turned to profit; for, lodging cheaply at the Shakespearian baker's, she roamed about, portfolio in hand, booking every lovely bit she saw, regardless of sun or rain, and bringing away a pictorial diary of that week's trip which charmed those who beheld it, and put money in her purse.

When the year was out, home came the artist, with half her little fortune still unspent, and the one trunk nearly as empty as it went, but there were two great boxes of pictures, and a golden saint in a coffin five feet long, which caused much interest at the Custom House, but was passed duty-free after its owner had displayed it with enthusiastic explanations of its charms.

"They are only attempts and studies, you know, and I dare say you'll all laugh at them; but I feel that I *can* in time *do* something, so my year has not been wasted," said the modest damsel, as she set forth her work, glorifying all the house with Venetian color, English verdure, and, what was better still, the sunshine of a happy heart.

But to B's great surprise and delight, people did *not* laugh; they praised and bought, and ordered more, till, before she knew it, several thousand dollars were at her command, and the way clear to the artist-life she loved.

To some who watched her, the sweetest picture she created was the free art-school which B opened in a very humble way; giving her books, copies, casts, time, and teaching to all who cared to come. For with her, as with most who *earn* their good things, the generous desire to share them with others is so strong it is sure to blossom out in some way, blessing as it has been blessed. Slowly, but surely, success comes to the patient worker, and B, being again abroad for more lessons, paints one day a little still life study so well that her master says she "does him honor," and her mâtes advise her to send it to the Salon. Never dreaming that it will be accepted, B, for the joke of it, puts her study in a plain frame, and sends it, with the eight thousand others, only two thousand of which are received.

To her amazement the little picture is accepted, hung "on the line" and noticed in the report. Nor is that all, the Committee asked leave to exhibit it at another place, and desired an autobiographical sketch of the artist. A more deeply gratified young woman it would be hard to find than B, as she now plans the studio she is to open soon, and the happy independent life she hopes to lead in it, for she has earned her place, and, after years of earnest labor, is about to enter in and joyfully possess it.

There was C,—alas, that I must write *was!* beautiful, gifted, young, and full of the lovely possibilities which give some girls such an indescribable charm. Placed where it would have been natural for her to have made herself a young queen of society, she preferred something infinitely better, and so quietly devoted herself to the chosen work that very few guessed she had any.

I had known her for some years before I found it out, and then only by accident; but I never shall forget the impression it made upon me. I had called to get a book, and something led me to speak of the sad case of a poor girl lately made known to me, when C, with a sudden brightening of her whole face, said, warmly, "I wish I had known it, I could have helped her."

"You? what can a happy creature like you know about such things?" I answered, surprised.

"That is my work." And in a few words which went to my heart, the beautiful girl, sitting in her own pretty room, told me how, for a long time, she and others had stepped out of their safe, sunshiny homes to help and save the most forlorn of our sister women. So quietly, so tenderly, that only those saved knew who did it, and such loyal silence kept, that, even among the friends, the names of these unfortunates were not given, that the after life might be untroubled by even a look of reproach or recognition.

"Do not speak of this," she said. "Not that I am ashamed; but we are able to work better in a private way, and want no thanks for what we do."

I kept silence till her share of the womanly labor

of love, so delicately, dutifully done, was over. But I never saw that sweet face afterward without thinking how like an angel's it must have seemed to those who sat in darkness till she came to lift them up.

Always simply dressed, this young sister of charity went about her chosen task when others of her age and position were at play; happy in it, and unconsciously preaching a little sermon by her lovely life. Another girl, who spent her days reading novels and eating confectionery, said to me, in speaking of C,—

"Why doesn't she dress more? She is rich enough, and so handsome I should think she would."

Taking up the reports of several charities which lay on my table, I pointed to C's name among the generous givers, saying,—

"Perhaps *that* is the reason;" and my visitor went away with a new idea of economy in her frivolous head, a sincere respect for the beautiful girl who wore the plain suit and loved her neighbor *better* than herself.

A short life; but one so full of sweetness that all the bitter waters of the pitiless sea cannot wash its memory away, and I am sure that white soul won heaven sooner for the grateful prayers of those whom she had rescued from a blacker ocean.

D was one of a large family all taught at home, and all of a dramatic turn; so, with a witty father to write the plays, an indulgent mother to yield up her house to destruction, five boys and seven girls for the *corps dramatique*, it is not to be wondered at that D set her heart on being an actress.

Having had the honor to play the immortal Pillicoddy on that famous stage, I know whereof I write, and what glorious times that little company of brothers and sisters had safe at home. But D burned for a larger field, and at length found a chance to appear on the real boards with several of her sisters. Being very small and youthful in appearance they played children's parts, fairies in spectacles and soubrettes in farce or vaudeville. Once D had a benefit, and it was a pretty sight to see the long list of familiar names on the bill; for the brothers and sisters all turned out and made a jolly play of "Parents and Guardians," as well as a memorable sensation in the "Imitations" which they gave.

One would think that the innocent little girls might have come to harm singing in the chorus of operas, dancing as peasants, or playing "Nan the good-for-nothing." But the small women were so dignified, well-mannered, and intent on their duties that no harm befell them. Father and brothers watched over them; there were few temptations for girls who made "Mother" their confidante, and a happy home was a safe refuge from the unavoidable annoyances to which all actresses are exposed.

D tried the life, found it wanting, left it, and put her experiences into a clever little book, then turned to less pleasant but more profitable work. The father, holding a public office, was allowed two clerks; but, finding that his clear-headed daughter could do the work of both easily and well, gave her the place, and she earned her thousand a year, going to her daily duty looking like a school girl; while her brain was busy with figures and statistics which would have puzzled many older heads.

This she did for years, faithfully earning her salary, and meanwhile playing her part in the domestic drama; for real tragedy and comedy came into it as time went on; the sisters married or died, brothers won their way up, and more than one Infant Phenomenon appeared on the household stage.

But through all changes my good D was still "leading lady," and now, when the mother is gone,

the other birds all flown, she remains in the once overflowing nest, the stay and comfort of her father, unspoiled by either poverty or wealth, unsaddened by much sorrow, unsoured by spinsterhood. A wise and witty little woman, and a happy one too, though the curly locks are turning gray; for the three Christian graces, faith, hope, and charity, abide with her to the end.

Of E I know too little to do justice to her success; but as it has been an unusual one, I cannot resist giving her a place here, although I never saw her, and much regret that now I never can, since she has gone to plead her own cause before the wise Judge of all.

Her story was told me by a friend, and made so strong an impression upon me that I wrote down the facts while they were fresh in my mind. A few words, added since her death, finish the too brief record of her brave life.

At fourteen, E began to read law with a legal friend. At eighteen she began to practise, and did so well that this friend offered her half his business, which was very large. But she preferred to stand alone, and in two years had a hundred cases of all sorts in different courts, and never lost one.

In a certain court-room, where she was the only woman present, her bearing was so full of dignity that every one treated her with respect. Her opponent, a shrewd old lawyer, made many sharp or impertinent remarks, hoping to anger her and make her damage her cause by some loss of self-control. But she merely looked at him with such a wise, calm smile, and answered with such unexpected wit and wisdom, that the man was worsted and young Portia won her suit, to the great satisfaction of the spectators, men though they were.

She used to say that her success was owing to hard work, — too hard, I fear, if she often studied eighteen hours a day. She asked no help or patronage, only fair play, and one cannot but regret that it ever was denied a creature who so womanfully proved her claim to it.

A friend says, "she was a royal girl, and did all her work in a royal way. She broke down suddenly, just as she had passed the last hostile outpost; just as she had begun to taste the ineffable sweetness of peace and rest, following a relative life-time of battle and toil."

But, short as her career has been, not one brave effort is wasted, since she has cleared the way for those who come after her, and proved that women have not only the right but the ability to sit upon the bench as well as stand at the bar of justice.

Last, but by no means least, is F, because her success is the most wonderful of all, since every thing was against her from the first, as you will see when I tell her little story.

Seven or eight years ago, a brave woman went down into Virginia with a friend, and built a school-house for the freed people, who were utterly forlorn; because, though the great gift of liberty was theirs, it was so new and strange they hardly understood how to use it. These good women showed them, and among the first twenty children who began the school, which now has hundreds of pupils, white as well as black, came little F.

Ignorant, ragged and wild, yet with such an earnest, resolute face that she attracted the attention of her teachers at once, and her eagerness to learn touched their hearts; for it was a hard fight with her to get an education, because she could only be spared now and then from corn-planting, pulling fodder, toting water, oyster-shucking or grubbing the new land.

She must have made good use of those "odd days," for she was among the first dozen who earned a pictorial pocket-handkerchief for learning the multiplication table, and a proud child was F when she bore home the prize. Rapidly the patient little fingers learned to write on the first slate she ever saw, and her whole heart went into the task of reading the books which opened a new world to her.

The instinct of progression was as strong in her as the love of light in a plant, and when the stone was lifted away, she sprang up and grew vigorously.

At last the chance to go North and earn something, which all freed people desire, came to F; and in spite of many obstacles she made the most of it. At the very outset she had to fight for a place in the steamer, since the captain objected to her being admitted to the cabin on account of her color; though any lady could take her black maid in without any trouble. But the friend with whom she travelled insisted on F's rights, and won them by declaring that if the child was condemned to pass the night on deck, she would pass it with her.

F watched the contest with breathless interest, as well she might; for this was her first glimpse of the world outside the narrow circle where her fourteen years had been spent. Poor little girl! there seemed to be no place for her anywhere; and I cannot help wondering what her thoughts were, as she sat alone in the night, shut out from among her kind for no fault but the color of her skin.

What could she think of "white folks'" religion, intelligence, and courtesy? Fortunately she had one staunch friend beside her to keep her faith in human justice alive, and win a little place for her among her fellow beings. The captain for very shame consented at last, and F felt that she was truly free when she stepped out of the lonely darkness of the night into the light and shelter of the cabin, a harmless little girl, asking only a place to lay her head.

That was the first experience, and it made a deep impression on her; but those that followed were pleasanter, for nowhere in the free North was she refused her share of room in God's world.

I saw her in New York, and even before I learned her story I was attracted to the quiet, tidy, door-girl by the fact that she was always studying as she sat in the noisy hall of a great boarding-house, keeping her books under her chair and poring over them at every leisure moment. Kindly people, touched by her patient efforts, helped her along; and one of the prettiest sights I saw in the big city was a little white girl taking time from her own sports to sit on the stairs and hear F recite. I think Bijou Heron will never play a sweeter part than that, nor have a more enthusiastic admirer than F was when we went together to see the child-actress play "The Little Treasure" for charity.

To those who know F it seems as if a sort of miracle had been wrought, to change in so short a time a forlorn little Topsy into this intelligent, independent, ambitious girl, who not only supports and educates herself, but sends a part of her earnings home, and writes such good letters to her mates that they are read aloud in school. Here is a paragraph from one which was a part of the Christmas festival last year: —

"I have now seen what a great advantage it is to have an education. I begin to feel the good of the little I know, and I am trying hard every day to add more to it. Most every child up here from ten to twelve years old can read and write, colored as well as white. And if you were up here, I think you would be surprised to see such little bits of children going to school with their arms full of books. I do hope you will all learn as much as you can; for an Education is a great thing."

I wonder how many white girls of sixteen would do any better, if as well, as this resolute F, bravely making her way against fate and fortune, toward the useful, happy womanhood we all desire. I know she will find friends, and I trust that if she ever knocks at the door of any college, asking her sisters to let her in, they will not disgrace themselves by turning their backs upon her; but prove themselves worthy of their blessings, by showing them Christian gentlewomen.

Here are my six girls; doctor, artist, philanthropist, actress, lawyer, and freedwoman; only a few among the hundreds who work and win, and receive their reward, seen of men or only known to God. Perhaps some other girl reading of these may take heart again, and travel on cheered by their example; for the knowledge of what has been done often proves wonderfully inspiring to those who long to do.

I felt this strongly when I went to a Woman's Congress not long ago; for on the stage was a noble array of successful women, making the noblest use of their talents in discussing all the questions which should interest and educate their sex. I was particularly proud of the senators from Massachusetts, and, looking about the crowded house to see how the audience stirred and glowed under their inspiring words, I saw a good omen for the future.

Down below were grown people, many women, and a few men; but up in the gallery, like a garland of flowers, a circle of girlish faces looked down eager-eyed; listening, with quick smiles and tears, to the wit or eloquence of those who spoke, dropping their school books to clap heartily when a good point was made, and learning better lessons in those three days than as many years of common teaching could give them.

It was close and crowded down below, dusty and dark; but up in the gallery the fresh October air blew in, mellow sunshine touched the young heads, there was plenty of room to stir, and each day the garland seemed to blossom fuller and brighter, showing how the interest grew. There they were, the future Mary Livermores, Ednah Cheneys, Julia Howes, Maria Mitchells, Lucy Stones, unconsciously getting ready to play their parts on the wider stage which those pioneers have made ready for them, before gentler critics, a wiser public, and more enthusiastic friends.

Looking from the fine gray heads which adorned the shadowy platform, to the bright faces up aloft, I wanted to call out, —

"Look, listen, and learn, my girls; then, bringing your sunshine and fresh air, your youth and vigor, come down to fill nobly the places of these true women, and earn for yourselves the same success which will make their names long loved and honored in the land."

II.

LOST IN A LONDON FOG.

WE had been to tea with some friends in Shaftesbury Terrace, and were so busy with our gossip that the evening slipped away unperceived till the clock struck half-past ten. We were two lone ladies, and had meant to leave early, as we were strangers in London and had some way to drive; so our dismay on discovering the lateness of the hour may be imagined.

We had not engaged a carriage to come for us, knowing that a cab-stand was near by, and that a cab would be much cheaper than the snug broughams ladies usually secure for evening use.

Out flew the little maid to get us a cab, and we hurried on our wraps eager to be gone. But we waited and waited, for Mary Ann did not come, and we were beginning to think something had happened to her, when she came hurrying back to say that all the cabs were gone from the neighboring stand, and she had run to another, where, after some delay, she had secured a hansom.

Now it is not considered quite the thing for ladies to go about in hansom cabs, without a gentleman to accompany them, especially in the evening; but being independent Americans, and impatient to relieve our weary hostess of our presence, we said nothing, but bundled in, gave the address, — 24 Colville Gardens, Bayswater, — and away we went.

A dense fog had come on, and nothing was visible but a short bit of muddy street, and lamps looming dimly through the mist. Our driver was as husky as if it had got into his throat, and the big, white horse looked absolutely ghostly as he went off at the breakneck pace which seems as natural to the London cab-horse as mud is to London streets.

"Isn't it fun to go rattling round in this all-out-of-doors style, through a real London fog?" said my sister, who was now enjoying her first visit to this surprising city.

"That remains to be seen. For my part, I 'd give a good deal to be shut up, dry and decent, in a four-wheeler, this is so very rowdy," I returned, feeling much secret anxiety as to the propriety of our proceeding.

"You are sure you gave the man the right direction?" I asked, after we had driven through what seemed a wilderness of crescents, terraces, gardens and squares.

"Of course I did, and he answered, 'All right, mum.' Shall I ask him if it is all right?" said M, who dearly liked to poke up the little door in the roof, which was our only means of communication with the burly, breezy cherub who sat up aloft to endanger the life of his fare.

"You may, for we have ridden long enough to go to St. Paul's."

Up went the little door, and M asked blandly, —

"Are you sure you are going right, driver?"

"No, mum, I ain't," was the cheering response breathed through the trap-door (as M called it) in a hoarse whisper.

"I told you where to go, and it is time we were there."

"I'm new come to London, mum, and ain't used to these parts yet," — began the man.

"Good gracious! so are we; and I'm sure I can't tell you any thing more than the name and number I have already given. You'd better ask the first policeman we meet," cried I, with the foreboding fear heavier than before.

"All right, mum," and down went the little door, and off rattled the cab.

My irrepressible sister burst out laughing at the absurdity of our position.

"Don't laugh, M, for mercy's sake! It 's no joke to be wandering about this great city at eleven o'clock at night in a thick fog, with a tipsy driver," I croaked, with a warning pinch.

"He isn't tipsy, only stupid, as we are, not to have engaged a carriage to come for us."

"He is tipsy; I smelt gin in his breath, and he is half asleep up there, I 've no doubt, for we have passed one, if not two policemen, I 'm sure."

"Nonsense! you wouldn't know your own father in this mist. Let Jarvey alone and he will bring us safely home."

"We shall see," I answered, grimly, as a splash of mud lit upon my nose, and the cab gave a perilous lurch in cutting round a sharp corner.

Did any one ever find a policeman when he was wanted? I never did, though they are as thick as blackberries when they are not needed.

On and on we went, but not a felt helmet appeared, and never did escaping fugitive look more eagerly for the North Star than I did for a gleaming badge on a blue coat.

"There 's a station! I shall stop and ask, for I 'm not going slamming and splashing about any longer.

Hi there, driver!" and I poked up the door with a vigor that would have startled the soundest sleeper.

"Ay, ay, mum," came the wheezy whisper, more wheezy than ever.

"Stop at this station-house and hail some one. We *must* get home, and you *must* ask the way."

"All right, mum," came back the hollow mockery conveyed in those exasperating words.

We did stop, and a star did appear, when I, with all the dignity I could muster, stated the case and asked for aid.

"Pleeseman X," gave it civilly; but I greatly fear he did not believe that the muddy-faced woman with a croaky voice, and the blonde damsel with curls, long earrings and light gloves, were really respectable members of the glorious American Republic.

I felt this and I could not blame him; so, thanking him with a bow which would have done credit to the noblest of my Hancock and Quincy ancestors, we went on again.

Alas, alas, it was all go on and no stop; for although our driver had responded briskly, "Ay, ay, sir," to the policeman's inquiry, "You know your way now, don't you?" he evidently did not know it, and the white horse went steadily up and down the long, wet streets, like a phantom steed in a horrid dream.

Things really were becoming serious; midnight was approaching. I had not the remotest idea where we were, and the passers-by became more and more infrequent, lights vanished from windows, few cabs were seen and the world was evidently going to bed. The fog was rapidly extinguishing my voice, and anxiety quenching my courage. M's curls hung limp and wild about her face, and even M's spirits began to fail.

"I am afraid we *are* lost," she whispered in my ear.

"Not a doubt of it."

"The man *must* be tipsy, after all."

"That is evident."

"What *will* people think of us?"

"That we are tipsy also."

"What *shall* we do?"

"Nothing but sit here and drift about till morning. The man has probably tumbled off; this dreadful horse is evidently wound up and won't stop till he has run down; the fog is increasing, and nothing will bring us to a halt but a collision with some other shipwrecked Yankee, as lost and miserable as we are."

"Oh, L, don't be sarcastic and grim now! Do exert yourself and land somewhere. Go to a hotel. This horrid man must know where the Langham is."

"I doubt if he knows any thing, and I am sure that eminently respectable house would refuse to admit such a pair of frights as we are, at this disreputable hour. No, we must go on till something happens to save us. We have discovered the secret of perpetual motion, and that is some comfort."

M groaned, I laughed, the ghostly horse sneezed, and I think the driver snored.

When things are pretty comfortable I am apt to croak, but when every thing is tottering on the verge of annihilation I usually feel rather jolly. Such being the perversity of my fallen nature, I began to enjoy myself at this period, and nearly drove poor M out of her wits by awful or whimsical suggestions and pictures of our probable fate.

It was so very absurd that I really could not help seeing the funny side of the predicament, and M was the best fun of all, she looked so like a dilapidated Ophelia with her damp locks, a blue rigolette all awry, her white gloves tragically clasped, and her pale countenance bespattered with the mud that lay thick on the wooden boot and flew freely from the wheels.

I had my laugh out and then tried to mend matters. What could we do? My first impulse was to stir up the sleeping wretch above, and this I did by energetically twitching the reins that hung loosely before our noses like the useless rudder of this lost ship.

"Young man, if you don't wake up and take us to Colville Gardens as quickly as possible, I shall report you to-morrow. I 've got your number, and I shall get my friend, Mr. Peter Taylor, of Aubrey House, to attend to the matter. He 's an M. P., and will see that you are fined for attempting to drive a cab when you know nothing of London."

I fear that most of this impressive harangue was lost, owing to the noise of the wheels and the feebleness of my nearly extinguished voice; but it had some effect, for though the man did not seem scared by the threatened wrath of an M. P., he did feel his weak point and try to excuse it, for he answered in a gruffy, apologetic tone, —

"Who 's a-goin' to know any thing in such a blessed fog as this? Most cabbies wouldn't try to drive at no price, but I'll do my best, mum."

"Very well. Do you know where we are now?" I demanded.

"Blest if I do!"

He didn't say "blest" — quite the reverse; — but I forgave him, for he really did seem to be making an effort, having had his nap out. An impressive pause followed, then M had an inspiration.

"Look, there's a respectable man just going into his house from that four-wheeled cab. Let us hail the whole concern, and get help of some sort."

I gave the order, and, eager to be rid of us at any price, our man rattled us up to the door at which a gray-haired gentleman was settling with his driver.

Bent on clutching this spar of salvation, I burst out of our cab and hastened up to the astonished pair. What I said I don't know, but vaguely remember jumbling into my appeal all the names of all the celebrated and respectable persons whom I knew on both sides of the water, for I felt that my appearance was entirely against me, and really expected to be told to go about my business.

John Bull, however, had pity upon me, and did his best for us, like a man and a brother.

"Take this cab, madam; the driver knows what he is about, and will see you safely home. I'll attend to the other fellow," said the worthy man, politely ignoring my muddy visage and agitated manners.

Murmuring blessings on his head, we skipped into

the respectable four-wheeler, and in a burst of confidence I offered Mr. Bull my purse to defray the expenses of our long drive.

"Rash woman, you'll never see your money again!" cried M, hiding her Roman earrings and clutching her Etruscan locket, prepared for highway robbery if not murder.

I did see my purse again and my money, also; for that dear old gentleman paid our miserable cabby out of his own pocket (as I found afterwards), and with a final gruff "All right!" the pale horse and his beery driver vanished in the mist. It is, and always will be my firm belief that it was a phantom cab, and that it is still revolving ceaselessly about London streets, appearing and disappearing through the fog, to be hailed now and then by some fated passenger, who is whisked to and fro, bewildered and forlorn, till rescued, when ghostly steed and phantom cab vanish darkly.

"Now you will be quite safe, ladies;" and the good old gentleman dismissed us with a paternal smile.

With a feeling of relief I fell back, exhausted by our tribulations.

"I know now how the wandering Jew felt," said M, after a period of repose.

"I don't wish to croak, dear; but if this man does not stop soon, I shall begin to think we have gently stepped out of the frying-pan into the fire. Unless we were several miles out of our way, we ought to arrive *somewhere*," I responded, flattening my nose against the pane, though I literally could not see one inch before that classical feature.

"Well, I'm so tired, I shall go to sleep, whatever happens, and you can wake me up when it is time to scream or run," said M, settling herself for a doze.

I groaned dismally, and registered a vow to spend all my substance in future on the most elegant and respectable broughams procurable for money, with a gray-haired driver pledged to temperance, and a stalwart footman armed with a lantern, pistol, directory, and map of London.

All of a sudden the cab stopped; the driver, not being a fixture, descended, and coming to the window, said, civilly, —

"The fog is so thick, mum, I'm not quite sure if I'm right, but this is Colville Square."

"Don't know any such place. Colville Gardens is what we want. There's a church at the end, and trees in the middle, and" —

"No use, mum, describin' it, for I can't see a

thing. But the Gardens can't be far off, so I 'll try again."

"We never shall find it, so we had better ask the man to take us at once to some station, work-house, or refuge till morning," remarked M, in such a tone of sleepy resignation that I shook her on the spot.

Another jaunt up and down, fog getting thicker, night later, one woman sleepier and the other crosser every minute, but still no haven hove in sight. Presently the cab stopped with a decided bump against the curb-stone, and the driver reappeared, saying, with respectful firmness, —

"My horse is beat out, and it 's past my time for turning in, so if this ain't the place I shall have to give it up, mum."

"It is *not* the place," I answered, getting out with the calmness of despair.

"There 's a light in that house and a woman looking out. Go and ask her where we are," suggested M, waking from her doze.

Ready now for any desperate measure, I rushed up the steps, tried vainly to read the number, but could not, and rang the bell with the firm determination to stay in that house till morning at any cost.

Steps came running down, the door flew open,

and I was electrified at beholding the countenance of my own buxom landlady.

"My dear soul, where 'ave you been?" she cried, as I stood staring at her, dumb with surprise and relief.

"From the Crystal Palace to Greenwich, I believe. Come in, M, and ask the man what the fare is," I answered, dropping into a hall chair, and feeling as I imagine Robinson Crusoe did when he got home.

Of course that civil cabby cheated me abominably. I knew it at the time, but never protested; for I was so glad and grateful at landing safely I should have paid a pound if he had asked it.

Next day we were heroines, and at breakfast alternately thrilled and convulsed the other boarders by a recital of our adventures. But the "strong-minded Americans" got so well laughed at that they took great care never to ride in hansom cabs again, or get lost in the fog.

III.

THE BOYS' JOKE, AND WHO GOT THE BEST OF IT.

IT was the day before Christmas, and grandpa's big house was swarming with friends and relations, all brimful of spirits and bent on having a particularly good time. Dinner was over and a brief lull ensued, during which the old folks took naps, the younger ones sat chatting quietly, while the children enlivened the day by a quarrel.

It had been brewing for some time, and during that half hour the storm broke. You see, the boys felt injured because for a week at least the girls had been too busy to pay the slightest attention to them and their affairs,—and what's the good of having sisters and cousins if they don't make themselves useful and agreeable to a fellow? What made it particularly hard to bear was the fact that there was a secret about it, and all they could discover was that *they* were to have no part in the fun. This added to their wrath, for they could have borne the temporary neglect, if the girls had been making something nice for *them;* but they were not, and the irate lads were coolly informed that they would never know the secret, or benefit by it in the least.

Now this sort of thing was not to be borne, you know, and after affecting to scorn the whole concern, the boys were finally goaded to confess to one another that they were dying to learn what was going on, though no power on earth would make them own as much to the girls. It certainly was very tantalizing to the poor fellows penned up in the breakfast-room (to keep the house quiet for an hour) to see the girls prance in and out of the library with the most aggravating air of importance and delight; to watch mysterious parcels borne along; to hear cries of rapture, admiration, or alarm from the next room, and to know that fun of some sort was going on, and they not in it.

It snowed so they could not go out; all had played their parts manfully at dinner, and were just in the lazy mood when a man likes to be amused by the gentler half of the race (which they believe was created for that express purpose), and there, on the other side of the folding doors, were half-a-dozen sprightly damsels, laughing and chatting, without a thought or care for the brothers and cousins gaping and growling close by.

The arrival of a sleigh-load of girlish neighbors added to the excitement, and made the boys feel that something must be done to redress their wrongs.

"Let 's burst in on them and take a look, no matter if they do scold," proposed Tom, the scapegrace, ready for a raid.

"No, that won't do; grandma said we were to let the girls alone, and we shall lose our presents if we don't behave. You just lean up against the door, Joe, and if it flies open, why it is an accident, you know," said Alf the wise.

So Joe, the fat cousin, backed up to the door like a young elephant, and leaned hard; but it was locked, and nothing came of it but a creak from the door, and a groan from Joe.

"I'll look through the keyhole, and tell what I see," cried little Neddy; and no one forbade him, though, at any other time, big brother Frank would have cuffed his ears for daring to suggest such a prank.

"There 's something bright, and the girls are fussing round it. Kitty 's got a lot of red and blue ribbons in her hand, and Grace is up in a chair, and Nell — oh, it 's cake; a great dish full of the jolliest kinds, and bon-bons, and sugared fruit, just the sort I like. I say, knock the door down, some of you big fellows, and let 's have one grab!" cried Neddy, maddened by the sight of the forbidden sweeties.

"Be quiet, and take another peep; it 's rather interesting to hear what 's going on," said Frank, reposing upon the sofa like the Great Mogul, as the boys called him.

Poor little Tantalus obediently applied his eye to the keyhole, but fell back with a blank face, saying in a despairing tone:

"They 've plugged it up, and I can't see a thing!"

"Serves you right; if you 'd held your tongue they never would have known what you were about," was Frank's ungrateful answer.

A stifled giggle from the other side of the door caused a dead silence to pervade the breakfast-room for several minutes, while Neddy wriggled out of sight under the sofa as if to escape from the finger of scorn.

Suddenly Tom cried in a shrill whisper, "I 've got it!" and pointed to a ventilator over the door.

A simultaneous rush of boys and chairs took place; but Tom claimed the rights of a discoverer, and, softly mounting an improvised ladder of tables and stools, he peered eagerly through the glass, while impatient hands plucked at his legs, and the pressure of the mob caused his perch to totter perilously.

The spectacle which he beheld would have touched the heart of any little girl, but to an unappreciative boy it possessed no charm, for it was only a doll's Christmas tree. For weeks, the young mammas had been making pretty things for their wooden, wax, or porcelain darlings, and it was excellent practice, since many a pair of hands that scorned patchwork and towels, labored patiently over small gowns, trimmed gay hats, and wrought wonders in worsted, without a sigh.

It really was a most delightful little tree, set in an Indian jar, snowed over with flour, garlanded with alternate festoons of cranberries and pop-corn, and every bough laden with such treasures that if dolls could stare any harder than they do, they certainly would have opened their painted eyes with amazement and joy. Such "darling" hats, and caps; such "sweet" gowns and cloaks; such "cunning" muffs and tippets! Dressing cases as perfect as grown-up ones, I assure you; mittens that must have been knit on darning-needles; shoes of colored kid fit for a doll's Cinderella, and sets of brass and bead jewelry that glittered splendidly. Wee bottles of perfume for waxen noses; tiny horns of comfits; travelling bags, and shawl straps, evidently worked by the fairies; and underclothes which I modestly forbear to describe, merely saying that very few of the seams were puckered, and the trimmings "perfectly lovely."

At the moment when Peeping Tom's profane eye beheld the innocent revel, the dolls were seated in a circle, their mammas standing behind them, while the happy little hostesses bestowed the gifts with appropriate remarks. It is needless to say that the dolls behaved beautifully, their cheeks glowing with pleasure as they returned thanks in voices so like those of their mothers that one couldn't tell the difference.

The tree was soon stripped, and then the chatter began again, for every thing must be tried on at once, and more than one doll who came in shabby clothes bloomed out in gorgeous array, or was made tidy for the winter.

"I'm so glad to get a worked flannel petticoat for

my Jemima. Mamma was saying only yesterday that she didn't approve of show at the expense of comfort, and I knew she meant Jemmy, who hadn't a thing on but her pink silk dress and ear-rings," observed Mrs. Kitty, in a moral tone.

"Clementina has been suffering for shoes, though her feet don't show with a train. I meant to have saved enough to buy her some, but what with limes and candy, and pencils, and fines for saying 'awful,' I do believe the poor thing would have gone bare-footed all winter, if Nell hadn't given her these beauties," replied Mrs. Alice, proudly surveying her daughter's feet in red kid boots of a somewhat tri-angular shape.

"I couldn't make them fit very well, because the cotton is all coming out of her toes, and it was hard to measure," explained Mrs. Nell, conscious that shoemaking was not her mission.

"They are just the thing; for I'm afraid my poor Clem is going to have the gout, young as she is. It is in our family, so it is well to be prepared," answered Mrs. Alice, with the beautiful forethought of a maternal heart.

"These muffs are made out of our Tabby's skin. I thought you'd like them as keepsakes, for we all loved her," said Grace, with a pensive sigh, as she smoothed the white fur of a dear departed cat, feeling that black and violet bows would have been more suitable than red and blue for the decoration of these touching memorials.

"I wonder if there isn't a nice place somewhere for good cats when they die? I hope so: for I'm sure they have souls, though they may be little bits of ones," observed Kitty, who felt as if her name was a tie between herself and the pets she most adored.

"I wonder if they have ghosts," said Nell, as if she feared that Tabby's might appear.

A faint "Meou" seemed to float down to the startled girls from some upper region, and for an instant they stood staring about them. Then they laughed like a chime of bells, and accused little Lotty of pinching the kitten in her arms.

"I didn't; it was Tom up dere," protested the child, pointing to the ventilator, from which a round red face was staring at them, like a full moon.

Shrieks of indignation greeted the discovery, and a rain of small articles pelted the countenance of the foe, as it grinned derisively, while a jeering voice called out:

"I don't think much of your old secret. It wasn't

worth the fuss you made about it, and I wouldn't have any if I couldn't do better than that."

"I 'd like to see you get up any thing half as nice. You couldn't do it. Boys never invent new games, but girls do. Papa says so, and he knows," answered Nell.

"Pooh! We fellows could beat you as easy as not, if we cared to; so you needn't brag, miss. Men invent every thing in the world, 'specially ventilators, and you see how useful they are," returned Tom, glad that he had kept his place in spite of the maltreatment his extremities were undergoing.

"Boys are more curious than girls, anyway. *We* should never have done such a mean thing as to peek at you," cried Kitty, coming to the rescue, and hitting the enemy in his weakest spot.

"Oh, we only did it for fun. Give us a taste of your spread, and we 'll never say a word about it," returned the barefaced boy, with a wheedlesome air, and a tender glance toward the dainty tea-table set forth so temptingly just under his nose.

"Not a bit, unless you 'll say our tree is lovely and own that we are the cleverest at getting up new and nice things," said Kitty, sternly.

"Never!" roared Tom; "we can beat you any day if we choose."

"Then do it, and we will own up; yes, and we will go halves in all the goodies we get off our big tree to-night," added Kitty, bound to stand by her sex and ready to wager a year's bon-bons in the defence of her position.

"By George, I'll do it if the fellows will agree! Honor bright now, and no dodging," said Tom, recklessly pledging himself and friends to any thing and every thing.

"Honor bright," chorused the girls in high glee.

"Only don't be a month about it; you boys are *so* slow," added Grace, in a superior tone, that ruffled the gentleman at the ventilator.

"We'll do it to-morrow; see if we don't," he cried out, rashly heaping difficulties upon his party.

"Then you'd better set about it at once, and leave us in peace," said Nell, tartly.

"I shall go, ma'am, when I please, and not one minute sooner"—began Tom, with immense dignity; but he did not keep his word; for the sudden withdrawal of his head, followed by a crash and howls of mingled merriment, wrath, and pain, plainly proved that circumstances over which he had no control hastened his departure.

The ladies sat down to their afternoon tea, which was much enlivened by guessing what those "stupid boys" would do. The gentlemen, warned by Tom's downfall, contented themselves with racking their mighty minds to invent some new, striking, and appropriate entertainment which should cover their names with glory and demolish their opponents for ever more.

Perhaps it was too soon after dinner; perhaps the brightest wits of the party had been shaken by the fall, or the cold affected the inventive powers; for, rack as they would, those mighty minds refused to work.

"You ought to have given us more time; of course we can't get up any thing clever in one day and a half," grumbled Frank, much annoyed because all the rest looked to him and he had not an idea to offer.

"I wasn't going to have a parcel of girls crow over me. I'd blow myself up for a show before I'd let them do that," answered Tom, rubbing his bruised elbows with a grim and defiant glance toward the fatal ventilator, for he felt that he had got not only himself but his mates into a scrape.

"Don't worry, old fellows; time enough; sleep on it, and something capital will pop into somebody's noddle, see if it doesn't," counselled Alf, with a sage nod, as he went to discover who was sobbing in the hall.

Little Lotty sat on the fuzzy red mat, with a tortoise-shell kitten in her arms, her white pinafore full of candies, and her chubby face bedewed with tears.

"What 's the matter, Toddlekins?" asked Alf, in such a sympathetic tone that the afflicted infant poured forth her woes in one breath, with the brown eyes flashing through their tears and a dramatic gesture of the small hands that told the tale better than her broken words.

"De naughty, naughty girls turned out my Torty 'cause she hopped on de table and drinked de tea, and I comed too, and we is doing to have a kitmouse tee all ourselfs up in de nursery, so now!"

Alf laughed at her indignation, but dried her tears, and sent her away happy with a sprig of hemlock from the decorations of the hall. "Virtue is its own reward" proved true in this case; for as Alf went back to his mates he had an idea — such a superb one that it nearly took his breath away and caused him to break into a wild sort of jig, as he cried aloud — "I 've found it, boys; I 've found it!"

"Where? What? How?" asked the others, clinging to him as if they were shipwrecked mariners, and he a rope thrown out to them.

The idea was evidently a good one, for it was received with great applause, and everybody was interested at once in helping Alf elaborate his plan.

"Won't it be heaping coals of fire on their heads after the shabby way they have treated us?" said Tom, chuckling at the thought of the girls' remorse when the touching surprise in store for them should be revealed.

"But how the dickens shall we get enough m——?" began Frank, rather inclined to throw cold water on the affair because he was not the originator of it.

"Hush!" shouted Alf; then added in a melodramatic whisper, "If the girls hear that word we are lost. I 've planned how to manage that, but it will take time, and we 'd better begin at once, or there won't be enough you-know-whats to go round. Come upstairs; we can talk safely there without a pack of girls listening at the keyhole, as I know they are this identical minute."

Alf raised his voice at the last words, and the boys trooped off with derisive hoots; for a guilty rustle and a sudden outburst of conversation in the other room told them that their shot had hit somebody.

"I wish we hadn't dared them to do it; for they will be sure to get up some dreadful surprise. I shall be expecting it every minute, and that will make me so nervous I shall not enjoy myself a bit."

"I'm not afraid; they won't invent any thing to-night, so we may as well clear up and be ready for our tree," answered Kitty to Nell as they packed the dolls on the sofa to sleep while their mammas enjoyed themselves.

No need to tell about that evening, for every child knows what a Christmas tree is better than we can describe it, so we will skip into the next morning when the boys' joke came off.

The young folks usually slept late after their unwonted revelry by night, but, strange to relate, the lads were early astir. In fact, Mary, the cook, saw several small ghosts whisking up the back-stairs when she went down to kindle her fire, and curious sounds were heard in attic and cellar, store-room and closets.

Something very exciting was going on, and the elders were evidently in it, for, though several mammas were heard to cry out when certain mysterious things were shown them, they never said a word, but looked up bits of gay ribbon without a murmur; while the papas enjoyed the fun and lent a hand in the most delightful manner.

When the girls came down to the late breakfast they found notes under their napkins, inviting them to a surprise party in the drying room at eleven A. M.

"I didn't think they 'd be so quick. Shall you dare to go?" whispered Nell to Kitty as they compared notes and tried to make out the device on the seal, which was evidently intended for an animal of some sort.

"We must go, for we promised. Of course it won't amount to any thing, and we can keep our sweeties," answered Kitty, lovingly eying the pretty box of French bon-bons which she had so rashly staked.

"You 'll be sorry if you don't, for it is the completest thing you ever saw, and no end of fun in it," began Tom, assuming an ecstatic expression and smacking his lips.

"Hold your tongue and go to work, or we shall not be ready in time. We've got to trim all the *jigamarees*, hang the *thingummies* while they are fresh, and see that the basket of *treasures* arrives safely," said Alf, with such mysterious nods and smiles that the girls were instantly consumed by an intense curiosity to know what "thingummies" and "jigamarees" were, while "treasures" had such a rich sound that they began to hope the boys were really going to atone for the past by some splendid piece of generosity.

"Come punctually at eleven and bring your boxes with you; they will be a good deal lighter when you come down again;" with which cheering remark Frank led off his men, leaving the girls to watch the clock with anxious, yet eager eyes.

Their wonder and suspense was much increased by the fact that Lotty was sent for and carried off by an escort of two. Listening at the foot of the back-stairs they heard her little voice exclaim approvingly:

"Oh how funny! how berry nice!" then the door closed, and the girls heard no more.

As the clock struck, up marched seven young ladies, each with a bon-bon box under her arm and an eager sparkle in her eyes. As they paused at the door Tom's voice was heard saying, "I wish they'd hurry up, for I'm tired of this business and have had scratching enough."

"They are coming! Now mind, no scrambling till I give the word. Each fellow stand in his place, keep the bows right side up and hold tight, or there will be a dreadful piece of work," answered Alf, evidently giving last touches to the spectacle.

"They have borrowed Fred's monkey and are going to scare us; I know they are by what Tom said: and I hear a queer noise — don't you?" whispered Nell, clutching Grace's skirts.

"It cannot be any thing very bad or Lotty would cry. Steady, girls; I'm going to knock," and Kitty gave a bold "rat-tat-tat," which caused a sensation within.

The door opened, and Frank made his best bow as he said, with a flourish:

"Enter, ladies, and join us in the interesting festival which we have prepared at your desire. Take a look first, and then I will explain this charming scene if it is not clear to you."

No need to tell the girls to take a look; they had done that already; but it was evident that an explanation would be necessary, for they were quite mystified by the "charming scene;" and well they might be, for it was a curious one.

The middle of the room was adorned by a large tub, in which stood a small spruce tree hung with the oddest things that ever swung from a bough. Mice by their tails, bits of cheese, milk in small bottles, gay balls, loops of string, squares of red and blue flannel like little blankets, bundles of herbs tied with bright ribbons, and near the top hung a cage with several small white animals dancing about in it.

But funniest of all was the circle of boys around this remarkable tree, at the foot of which Lotty sat; for each held a cat or kitten in his arms decorated with a gorgeous bow; both boys and cats so absurdly solemn and ill at ease that after one look the girls burst into a gale of merriment.

"Glad you like it, ladies; we have done our best, and I flatter myself it is a pretty neat thing," began showman Frank, with a gratified air, while the other boys with difficulty restrained their charges from escaping to their mistresses.

"It's very funny, but what does it all mean?" asked Grace, wiping her eyes, and nodding to her own fat Jerry, whose yellow eyes appealed to her for aid.

"It is a Kitmouse tree, the first one ever known, prepared at great expense for this occasion, to prove that *we* can invent superior amusements, and entirely outdo other folks who shall be nameless."

"It isn't half so pretty as our tree was," said Kitty, as Frank paused for breath.

"But think how much more pleasure it will give; for cats can enjoy and dolls can't. These presents are useful and instructive; for we have not only food and drink, but catnip and cataplasms for the poor darlings, if they have catarrh or any other catastrophe of that sort; but here is a little catechism for the kits, and string for cats' cradles when they have learned their lessons. Cataracts of milk will flow from these bottles for their refreshment, and a catalogue of delicacies will be furnished free to any lady wishing to repeat this performance at a future time."

"Hurry up, and give Jerry a bite of something, or he 'll eat me," cried Tom, who had been silently struggling with his puss while Frank delivered the speech, which he considered a masterpiece of wit.

"If the ladies will sit upon the window-seats I

will give out the presents at once;" and Frank proceeded to do so, amid much merriment; for the kittens began at once to play with the balls, the cats to eat and drink, while the boys surveyed the scene with great satisfaction, and the girls applauded as the mice were handed round, one to each cat, as a delicate attention, though few were eaten.

The pussies behaved remarkably well, for the lads had wisely selected the most amiable ones they could find, and the six belonging to the house received them hospitably. Mother Bunch and her three kits did the honors, while Torty and Jerry tried to be polite, though aristocratic Torty arched her back at the half-starved little cat Neddy found in the street, and stout old Jerry growled to himself when Nell's pretty white Snowball took his mouse away.

Such a frolic as they had, boys and girls, cats and kittens, altogether, one would have thought the house was coming down about their ears. The elders took a peep at them, but a very little of that sort of fun satisfied them and they soon left the youngsters to themselves.

"It's almost one, and we are going coasting before dinner, so own up girls, and hand over the goodies," said Alf at last, when a lull came and every one stopped for breath after a lively game of tag, which caused the cats to seek refuge in every available nook and corner.

"I suppose we must; for it certainly *was* a bright idea, and we have had a capital time," confessed honest Nell, sitting down in the clothes-basket, where Mother Bunch had collected her family when the romp began, and beginning to divide her candies.

"Stop a minute!" cried Kitty, with a twinkle in her black eyes; "was not the agreement that you should *invent* something newer and nicer than our dolls' affair?"

"Yes; and isn't this ever so much better fun in every way than all that fuss for rag babies that don't know or care any thing about it?" cried Alf, as proud as a peacock of his success.

"Of course it is," admitted sly Kitty.

"Wasn't it clever of us to get it up, and haven't we pleased you by treating your cats well?"

"I'm sure you have, and it was dear of you to do it."

"Well, then, what's the trouble?"

"Only that you did *not* invent the thing all yourselves," coolly answered Kitty.

"I should like to know who did!" cried the boys with one breath.

"Lotty. She put the idea into your heads with her funny word 'kitmouse.' You never would have thought of it but for that. A girl helped you; and a very little one too; you had to call her in to make the cats mind, I'm sure, so you have lost your wager and we will keep our bon-bons, thank you."

Kitty made a low courtesy and stood crunching a delicious strawberry drop as she triumphantly surveyed the astounded boys, who looked as much taken aback as Antonio and his friends when Portia outwits Shylock in the famous court scene.

"She's got us there," murmured Frank, with an approving nod to his clever young sister.

"Oh, come; that's not fair; we had a right to take just a word that meant nothing till we made it. I don't care for the sweet stuff, but I'm not going to own that we are beaten!" cried Alf, in high dudgeon; for he had taken much credit to himself for this bright idea.

"You *must* own that a girl helped you. Do that fairly and I'll go halves, as we promised; for you *have* made a good joke out of Lotty's word," said Kitty, who was generous as well as just, and felt that the poor lads deserved some reward for their labor.

"All right, if the other fellows agree," returned Tom, helping himself to a handful of candy as he spoke; which cool performance had such a good effect upon the other boys that they all cried out, "We do! we do!" while Alf, swinging Lotty to his shoulder, marched away, singing at the top of his voice,

"Now cheer, boys, cheer,
With three times three,
Our little Lot,
And her kitmouse tree!"

IV.

ROSES AND FORGET-ME-NOTS.

I.

ROSES.

IT was a cold November storm, and every thing looked forlorn. Even the pert sparrows were draggle-tailed and too much out of spirits to fight for crumbs with the fat pigeons who tripped through the mud with their little red boots as if in haste to get back to their cosy home in the dove-cot.

But the most forlorn creature out that day was a small errand girl, with a bonnet-box on each arm, and both hands struggling to hold a big broken umbrella. A pair of worn-out boots let in the wet upon her tired feet; a thin cotton dress and an old shawl poorly protected her from the storm; and a faded hood covered her head.

The face that looked out from this hood was too pale and anxious for one so young; and when a sudden gust turned the old umbrella inside out with a crash, despair fell upon poor Lizzie, and she was so miserable she could have sat down in the rain and cried.

But there was no time for tears; so, dragging the dilapidated umbrella along, she spread her shawl over the bonnet-boxes and hurried down the broad street, eager to hide her misfortunes from a pretty young girl who stood at a window laughing at her.

She could not find the number of the house where one of the fine hats was to be left; and after hunting all down one side of the street, she crossed over, and came at last to the very house where the pretty girl lived. She was no longer to be seen; and, with a sigh of relief, Lizzie rang the bell, and was told to wait in the hall while Miss Belle tried the hat on.

Glad to rest, she warmed her feet, righted her umbrella, and then sat looking about her with eyes quick to see the beauty and the comfort that made the place so homelike and delightful. A small waiting-room opened from the hall, and in it stood many blooming plants, whose fragrance attracted Lizzie as irresistibly as if she had been a butterfly or bee.

Slipping in, she stood enjoying the lovely colors, sweet odors, and delicate shapes of these household spirits; for Lizzie loved flowers passionately; and just then they possessed a peculiar charm for her.

One particularly captivating little rose won her

heart, and made her long for it with a longing that became a temptation too strong to resist. It was so perfect; so like a rosy face smiling out from the green leaves, that Lizzie could *not* keep her hands off it, and having smelt, touched, and kissed it, she suddenly broke the stem and hid it in her pocket. Then, frightened at what she had done, she crept back to her place in the hall, and sat there, burdened with remorse.

A servant came just then to lead her upstairs; for Miss Belle wished the hat altered, and must give directions. With her heart in a flutter, and pinker roses in her cheeks than the one in her pocket, Lizzie followed to a handsome room, where a pretty girl stood before a long mirror with the hat in her hand.

"Tell Madame Tifany that I don't like it at all, for she hasn't put in the blue plume mamma ordered; and I won't have rose-buds, they are so common," said the young lady, in a dissatisfied tone, as she twirled the hat about.

"Yes, miss," was all Lizzie could say; for *she* considered that hat the loveliest thing a girl could possibly own.

"You had better ask your mamma about it, Miss Belle, before you give any orders. She will be up in a few moments, and the girl can wait," put in a maid, who was sewing in the anteroom.

"I suppose I must; but I *won't* have roses," answered Belle, crossly. Then she glanced at Lizzie, and said more gently, "You look very cold; come and sit by the fire while you wait."

"I 'm afraid I'll wet the pretty rug, miss; my feet are sopping," said Lizzie, gratefully, but timidly.

"So they are! Why didn't you wear rubber boots?"

"I haven't got any."

"I 'll give you mine, then, for I hate them; and as I never go out in wet weather, they are of no earthly use to me. Marie, bring them here; I shall be glad to get rid of them, and I 'm sure they 'll be useful to you."

"Oh, thank you, miss! I 'd like 'em ever so much, for I 'm out in the rain half the time, and get bad colds because my boots are old," said Lizzie, smiling brightly at the thought of the welcome gift.

"I should think your mother would get you warmer things," began Belle, who found something rather interesting in the shabby girl, with shy bright eyes, and curly hair bursting out of the old hood.

"I haven't got any mother," said Lizzie, with a pathetic glance at her poor clothes.

"I'm so sorry! Have you brothers and sisters?" asked Belle, hoping to find something pleasant to talk about; for she was a kind little soul.

"No, miss; I've got no folks at all."

"Oh, dear; how sad! Why, who takes care of you?" cried Belle, looking quite distressed.

"No one; I take care of myself. I work for Madame, and she pays me a dollar a week. I stay with Mrs. Brown, and chore round to pay for my keep. My dollar don't get many clothes, so I can't be as neat as I'd like." And the forlorn look came back to poor Lizzie's face.

Belle said nothing, but sat among the sofa cushions, where she had thrown herself, looking soberly at this other girl, no older than she was, who took care of herself and was all alone in the world. It was a new idea to Belle, who was loved and petted as an only child is apt to be. She often saw beggars and pitied them, but knew very little about their wants and lives; so it was like turning a new page in her happy life to be brought so near to poverty as this chance meeting with the milliner's girl.

"Aren't you afraid and lonely and unhappy?" she said, slowly, trying to understand and put herself in Lizzie's place.

"Yes; but it 's no use. I can't help it, and may be things will get better by and by, and I 'll have my wish," answered Lizzie, more hopefully, because Belle's pity warmed her heart and made her troubles seem lighter.

"What is your wish?" asked Belle, hoping mamma wouldn't come just yet, for she was getting interested in the stranger.

"To have a nice little room, and make flowers, like a French girl I know. It 's such pretty work, and she gets lots of money, for every one likes her flowers. She shows me how, sometimes, and I can do leaves first-rate; but" —

There Lizzie stopped suddenly, and the color rushed up to her forehead; for she remembered the little rose in her pocket and it weighed upon her conscience like a stone.

Before Belle could ask what was the matter, Marie came in with a tray of cake and fruit, saying:

"Here 's your lunch, Miss Belle."

"Put it down, please; I 'm not ready for it yet."

And Belle shook her head as she glanced at Lizzie, who was staring hard at the fire with such a troubled face that Belle could not bear to see it.

Jumping out of her nest of cushions, she heaped a plate with good things, and going to Lizzie, offered it, saying, with a gentle courtesy that made the act doubly sweet:

"Please have some; you must be tired of waiting."

But Lizzie could not take it; she could only cover her face and cry; for this kindness rent her heart and made the stolen flower a burden too heavy to be borne.

"Oh, don't cry so! Are you sick? Have I been rude? Tell me all about it; and if I can't do any thing, mamma can," said Belle, surprised and troubled.

"No; I'm not sick; I'm bad, and I can't bear it when you are so good to me," sobbed Lizzie, quite overcome with penitence; and taking out the crumpled rose, she confessed her fault with many tears.

"Don't feel so much about such a little thing as that," began Belle, warmly; then checked herself, and added, more soberly, "It *was* wrong to take it without leave; but it's all right now, and I'll give you as many roses as you want, for I know you are a good girl."

"Thank you. I didn't want it only because it was pretty, but I wanted to copy it. I can't get any for myself, and so I can't do my make-believe ones well. Madame won't even lend me the old ones in the store, and Estelle has none to spare for me, because I can't pay her for teaching me. She gives me bits of muslin and wire and things, and shows me now and then. But I know if I had a real flower I could copy it; so she'd see I did know something, for I try real hard. I'm *so* tired of slopping round the streets, I'd do any thing to earn my living some other way."

Lizzie had poured out her trouble rapidly; and the little story was quite affecting when one saw the tears on her cheeks, the poor clothes, and the thin hands that held the stolen rose. Belle was much touched, and, in her impetuous way, set about mending matters as fast as possible.

"Put on those boots and that pair of dry stockings right away. Then tuck as much cake and fruit into your pocket as it will hold. I'm going to get you some flowers, and see if mamma is too busy to attend to me."

With a nod and a smile, Belle flew about the room a minute; then vanished, leaving Lizzie to her comfortable task, feeling as if fairies still haunted the world as in the good old times.

When Belle came back with a handful of roses, she found Lizzie absorbed in admiring contemplation of her new boots, as she ate sponge-cake in a blissful sort of waking-dream.

"Mamma can't come; but I don't care about the hat. It will do very well, and isn't worth fussing about. There, will those be of any use to you?" And she offered the nosegay with a much happier face than the one Lizzie first saw.

"Oh, miss, they're just lovely! I'll copy that pink rose as soon as ever I can, and when I've learned how to do 'em tip-top, I'd like to bring you some, if you don't mind," answered Lizzie, smiling all over her face as she buried her nose luxuriously in the fragrant mass.

"I'd like it very much, for I should think you'd have to be very clever to make such pretty things. I really quite fancy those rose-buds in my hat, now I know that you're going to learn how to make them. Put an orange in your pocket, and the flowers in water as soon as you can, so they'll be fresh when you want them. Good by. Bring home our hats every time and tell me how you get on."

With kind words like these, Belle dismissed Lizzie, who ran downstairs, feeling as rich as if she had found a fortune. Away to the next place she hurried, anxious to get her errands done and the precious posy safely into fresh water. But Mrs. Turretville was not at home, and the bonnet could not be left till paid for. So Lizzie turned to go down the high steps, glad that she need not wait. She stopped one instant to take a delicious sniff at her flowers, and that was the last happy moment that poor Lizzie knew for many weary months.

The new boots were large for her, the steps slippery with sleet, and down went the little errand girl, from top to bottom, till she landed in the gutter directly upon Mrs. Turretville's costly bonnet.

"I 've saved my posies, anyway," sighed Lizzie, as she picked herself up, bruised, wet, and faint with pain; "but, oh, my heart! won't Madame scold when she sees that band-box smashed flat," groaned the poor child, sitting on the curbstone to get her breath and view the disaster.

The rain poured, the wind blew, the sparrows on the park railing chirped derisively, and no one came along to help Lizzie out of her troubles. Slowly she gathered up her burdens; painfully she limped away in the big boots; and the last the naughty sparrows saw of her was a shabby little figure going round the corner, with a pale, tearful face held lovingly over the bright bouquet that was her one treasure and her only comfort in the moment which brought to her the great misfortune of her life.

II.

FORGET-ME-NOTS.

"Oh, mamma, I am so relieved that the box has come at last! If it had not, I do believe I should have died of disappointment," cried pretty Belle, five years later, on the morning before her eighteenth birthday.

"It would have been a serious disappointment, darling; for I had set my heart on your wearing my gift to-morrow night, and when the steamers kept coming in without my trunk from Paris, I was very anxious. I hope you will like it."

"Dear mamma, I know I shall like it; your taste is so good and you know what suits me so well. Make haste, Marie; I'm dying to see it," said Belle, dancing about the great trunk, as the maid carefully unfolded tissue papers and muslin wrappers.

A young girl's first ball-dress is a grand affair,—in her eyes, at least; and Belle soon stopped dancing, to stand with clasped hands, eager eyes and parted lips before the snowy pile of illusion that was at last daintily lifted out upon the bed. Then, as Marie displayed its loveliness, little cries of delight were heard, and when the whole delicate dress was arranged to the best effect she threw herself upon her mother's neck and actually cried with pleasure.

"Mamma, it is too lovely! and you are very kind to do so much for me. How shall I ever thank you?"

"By putting it right on to see if it fits; and when you wear it look your happiest, that I may be proud of my pretty daughter."

Mamma got no further, for Marie uttered a French shriek, wrung her hands, and then began to burrow wildly in the trunk and among the papers, crying distractedly:

"Great heavens, madame! the wreath has been forgotten! What an affliction! Mademoiselle's enchanting toilette is destroyed without the wreath, and nowhere do I find it."

In vain they searched; in vain Marie wailed and Belle declared it must be somewhere; no wreath appeared. It was duly set down in the bill, and a fine sum charged for a head-dress to match the dainty forget-me-nots that looped the fleecy skirts and ornamented the bosom of the dress. It had evidently been forgotten; and mamma despatched Marie at once to try and match the flowers, for Belle would not hear of any other decoration for her beautiful blonde hair.

The dress fitted to a charm, and was pronounced by all beholders the loveliest thing ever seen. Nothing was wanted but the wreath to make it quite perfect, and when Marie returned, after a long search, with no forget-me-nots, Belle was in despair.

"Wear natural ones," suggested a sympathizing friend.

But another hunt among greenhouses was as fruitless as that among the milliners' rooms. No forget-me-nots could be found, and Marie fell exhausted into a chair, desolated at what she felt to be an awful calamity.

"Let me have the carriage, and I'll ransack the city till I find some," cried Belle, growing more resolute with each failure.

Mamma was deep in preparations for the ball, and could not help her afflicted daughter, though she was much disappointed at the mishap. So Belle drove off, resolved to have her flowers whether there were any or not.

Any one who has ever tried to match a ribbon, find a certain fabric, or get any thing done in a hurry, knows what a wearisome task it sometimes is, and can imagine Belle's state of mind after repeated disappointments. She was about to give up in despair, when some one suggested that perhaps the Frenchwoman, Estelle Valnor, might make the desired wreath, if there was time.

Away drove Belle, and, on entering the room, gave a sigh of satisfaction, for a whole boxful of the loveliest forget-me-nots stood upon the table. As fast as possible, she told her tale and demanded the flowers, no matter what the price might be. Imagine her feelings when the Frenchwoman, with a shrug, announced that it was impossible to give mademoiselle a single spray. All were engaged to trim a bridesmaid's dress, and must be sent away at once.

It really was too bad! and Belle lost her temper entirely, for no persuasion or bribes would win a spray from Estelle. The provoking part of it was that the wedding would not come off for several days, and there was time enough to make more flowers for that dress, since Belle only wanted a few for her hair. Neither would Estelle make her any, as her hands were full, and so small an order was not worth deranging one's self for; but observing Belle's sorrowful face, she said, affably:

"Mademoiselle may, perhaps, find the flowers she desires at Miss Berton's. She has been helping me with these garlands, and may have some left. Here is her address."

Belle took the card with thanks, and hurried away with a last hope faintly stirring in her girlish heart, for Belle had an unusually ardent wish to look her best at this party, since Somebody was to be there, and Somebody considered forget-me-nots the sweetest flowers in the world. Mamma knew this, and the kiss Belle gave her when the dress came had a more tender meaning than gratified vanity or daughterly love.

Up many stairs she climbed, and came at last to a little room, very poor but very neat, where, at the one window, sat a young girl, with crutches by her side and her lap full of flower-leaves and petals. She rose slowly as Belle came in, and then stood looking at her, with such a wistful expression in her shy, bright eyes, that Belle's anxious face cleared involuntarily, and her voice lost its impatient tone.

As she spoke, she glanced about the room, hoping to see some blue blossoms awaiting her. But none appeared; and she was about to despond again, when the girl said, gently:

"I have none by me now, but I may be able to find you some."

"Thank you very much; but I have been everywhere in vain. Still, if you do get any, please send them to me as soon as possible. Here is my card."

Miss Berton glanced at it, then cast a quick look at the sweet, anxious face before her, and smiled so brightly that Belle smiled also, and asked, wonderingly:

"What is it? What do you see?"

"I see the dear young lady who was so kind to me long ago. You don't remember me, and never knew my name; but I never have forgotten you all these years. I always hoped I could do something to show how grateful I was, and now I can, for you shall have your flowers if I sit up all night to make them."

But Belle still shook her head and watched the smiling face before her with wondering eyes, till the girl added, with sudden color in her cheeks:

"Ah, you 've done so many kind things in your life, you don't remember the little errand girl from Madame Tifany's who stole a rose in your hall, and how you gave her rubber boots and cake and flowers, and were so good to her she couldn't forget it if she lived to be a hundred."

"But you are so changed," began Belle, who did faintly recollect that little incident in her happy life.

"Yes, I had a fall and hurt myself so that I shall always be lame."

And Lizzie went on to tell how Madame had dismissed her in a rage; how she lay ill till Mrs. Brown sent her to the hospital; and how for a year she had suffered much alone, in that great house of pain, before one of the kind visitors had befriended her.

While hearing the story of the five years, that had been so full of pleasure, ease and love for herself, Belle forgot her errand, and, sitting beside Lizzie, listened with pitying eyes to all she told of her endeavors to support herself by the delicate handiwork she loved.

"I'm very happy now," ended Lizzie, looking about the little bare room with a face full of the sweetest content. "I get nearly work enough to pay my way, and Estelle sends me some when she has more than she can do. I've learned to do it nicely, and it is so pleasant to sit here and make flowers instead of trudging about in the wet with other people's hats. Though I do sometimes wish I was able to trudge, one gets on so slowly with crutches."

A little sigh followed the words, and Belle put her own plump hand on the delicate one that held the crutch, saying, in her cordial young voice:

"I'll come and take you to drive sometimes, for you are too pale, and you'll get ill sitting here at work day after day. Please let me; I'd love to; for I feel so idle and wicked when I see busy people like you that I reproach myself for neglecting my duty and having more than my share of happiness."

Lizzie thanked her with a look, and then said, in a tone of interest that was delightful to hear:

"Tell about the wreath you want; I should so love to do it for you, if I can."

Belle had forgotten all about it in listening to this sad little story of a girl's life. Now she felt half ashamed to talk of so frivolous a matter till she remembered that it would help Lizzie; and, resolving to pay for it as never garland was paid for before, she entered upon the subject with renewed interest.

"You shall have the flowers in time for your ball to-morrow night. I will engage to make a wreath that will please you, only it may take longer than I think. Don't be troubled if I don't send it till evening; it will surely come in time. I can work fast, and this will be the happiest job I ever did," said Lizzie, beginning to lay out mysterious little tools and bend delicate wires.

"You are altogether too grateful for the little I have done. It makes me feel ashamed to think I did not find you out before and do something better worth thanks."

"Ah, it wasn't the boots or the cake or the roses, dear Miss Belle. It was the kind looks, the gentle words, the way it was done, that went right to my heart, and did me more good than a million of money. I never stole a pin after that day, for the little rose wouldn't let me forget how you forgave me so sweetly. I sometimes think it kept me from greater temptations, for I was a poor, forlorn child, with no one to keep me good."

Pretty Belle looked prettier than ever as she listened, and a bright tear stood in either eye like a drop of dew on a blue flower. It touched her very much to learn that her little act of childish charity had been so sweet and helpful to this lonely girl, and now lived so freshly in her grateful memory. It showed her, suddenly, how precious little deeds of love and sympathy are; how strong to bless, how easy to perform, how comfortable to recall. Her heart was very full and tender just then, and the lesson sunk deep into it never to be forgotten.

She sat a long time watching flowers bud and blossom under Lizzie's skilful fingers, and then hurried home to tell all her glad news to mamma.

If the next day had not been full of most delightfully exciting events, Belle might have felt some anxiety about her wreath, for hour after hour went by and nothing arrived from Lizzie.

Evening came, and all was ready. Belle was dressed, and looked so lovely that mamma declared she needed nothing more. But Marie insisted that the grand effect would be ruined without the garland among the sunshiny hair. Belle had time now to be anxious, and waited with growing impatience for the finishing touch to her charming toilette.

"I must be downstairs to receive, and can't wait another moment; so put in the blue pompon and let me go," she said at last, with a sigh of disappointment; for the desire to look beautiful that night in Somebody's eyes had increased four-fold.

With a tragic gesture, Marie was about to adjust the pompon when the quick tap of a crutch came down the hall, and Lizzie hurried in, flushed and breathless, but smiling happily as she uncovered the box she carried with a look of proud satisfaction.

A general "Ah!" of admiration arose as Belle, mamma, and Marie surveyed the lovely wreath that lay before them; and when it was carefully arranged on the bright head that was to wear it, Belle blushed with pleasure. Mamma said: "It is more beautiful than any Paris could have sent us;" and Marie clasped her hands theatrically, sighing, with her head on one side:

"Truly, yes; mademoiselle is now adorable!"

"I am so glad you like it. I did my very best and worked all night, but I had to beg one spray from Estelle, or, with all my haste, I could not have finished in time," said Lizzie, refreshing her weary eyes with a long, affectionate gaze at the pretty figure before her.

A fold of the airy skirt was caught on one of the blue clusters, and Lizzie knelt down to arrange it as she spoke. Belle leaned toward her and said softly: "Money alone can't pay you for this kindness; so tell me how I can best serve you. This is the happiest night of my life, and I want to make every one feel glad also."

"Then don't talk of paying me, but promise that I may make the flowers you wear on your wedding-day," whispered Lizzie, kissing the kind hand held out to help her rise, for on it she saw a brilliant ring, and in the blooming, blushing face bent over her she read the tender little story that Somebody had told Belle that day.

"So you shall! and I'll keep this wreath all my life for your sake, dear," answered Belle, as her full heart bubbled over with pitying affection for the poor girl who would never make a bridal garland for herself.

Belle kept her word, even when she was in a happy home of her own; for out of the dead roses bloomed a friendship that brightened Lizzie's life;

and long after the blue garland was faded Belle remembered the helpful little lesson that taught her to read the faces poverty touches with a pathetic eloquence, which says to those who look, "Forget-me-not."

V.

OLD MAJOR.

"O MAMMA, don't let them kill him! He isn't doing any harm, and he's old and weak, and hasn't any one to be good to him but Posy and me!" cried little Ned, bursting into his mother's room, red and breathless with anxiety and haste.

"Kill whom, dear? Sit down and tell me all about it."

"I *can't* sit down, and I *must* be quick, for they may do it while I'm gone. I left Posy to watch him, and she is going to scream with all her might the minute she sees them coming back!" cried Ned, hovering restlessly about the doorway, as if expecting the call that was to summon him to the rescue.

"Mercy on us! what is it, child?"

"A dear old horse, mamma, who has been hobbling round the road for a week. I've seen him driven away from all the neighbors, so Posy and I give him clover and pat him; and to-day we found him at our bars, looking over at us playing in the field. I wanted him to come in, but Mr. White came along and drove him off, and said he was to be killed because he had no master, and was a nuisance. Don't let him do it!"

"But, Neddy, I cannot take him in, as I did the lame chicken, and the cat without a tail. He is too big, and eats too much, and we have no barn. Mr. White can find his master, perhaps, or use him for light work."

Mamma got no further, for Ned said again,—

"No, he can't. He says the poor old thing is of no use but to boil up. And his master won't be found, because he has gone away, and left Major to take care of himself. Mr. White knew the man, and says he had Major more than eighteen years, and he was a good horse, and now he's left to die all alone. Wouldn't I like to pound that man?"

"It *was* cruel, Neddy, and we must see what we can do."

So mamma put down her work and followed her boy, who raced before her to tell Posy it would be "all right" now.

Mrs. West found her small daughter perched on a stone wall, patting the head of an old white horse, who looked more like a skeleton than a living animal. Ned gave a whoop as he came, and the poor beast hastily hobbled across the road, pressing himself into a nook full of blackberry vines and thorny barberry bushes, as if trying to get out of sight and escape tormentors.

"That's the way he does when any one comes, because the boys plague him, and people drive him about till he doesn't know what to do. Isn't it a pity to see him so, mamma?" said tender-hearted Ned, as he pulled a big handful of clover from his father's field close by.

Indeed, it was sad, for the poor thing had evidently been a fine horse once; one could see that by his intelligent eye, the way he pricked up his ears, and the sorrowful sort of dignity with which he looked about him, as if asking a little compassion in memory of his long faithfulness.

"See his poor legs all swelled up, and the bones in his back, and the burrs the bad boys put in his mane, and the dusty grass he has to eat. Look! he knows me, and isn't afraid, because I'm good to him," said Ned, patting old Major, who gratefully ate fresh clover from the friendly little hand.

"Yes, and he lets me stroke his nose, mamma.

It 's as soft as velvet, and his big eyes don't frighten me a bit, they are so gentle. Oh, if we could only put him in our field, and keep him till he dies, I should be so happy!" said Posy, with such a wheedlesome arm about mamma's neck, that it was very hard to deny her any thing.

"If you will let me have Major, I won't ask for any other birthday present," cried Ned, with a sudden burst of generosity, inspired, perhaps, by the confiding way in which the poor beast rubbed his gray head against the boy's shoulder.

"Why, Neddy, do you really mean that? I was going to give you something you want very much. Shall I take you at your word, and give you a worn-out old horse instead?" asked mamma, surprised, yet pleased at the offer.

Ned looked at her, then at old Major, and wavered; for he guessed that the other gift was the little wheelbarrow he had begged for so long,—the dear green one, with the delicious creak and rumble to it. He had seen it at the store, and tried it, and longed for it, and planned to trundle every thing in it, from Posy to a load of hay. Yes, it must be his, and Major must be left to his fate.

Just as he decided this, however, Posy gave a cry

that told him Mr. White was coming. Major pressed further into the prickly hedge, with a patient sort of sigh, and a look that went to Ned's heart, for it seemed to say, —

"Good by, little friend. Don't give up any thing for me. I'm not worth it, for I can only love you in return."

Mr. White was very near, but Major was safe; for, with a sudden red in his freckled cheeks, Ned put his arm on the poor beast's drooping neck, and said, manfully, —

"I choose *him*, mamma; and now he's mine, I'd like to see anybody touch him!"

It was a pretty sight, — the generous little lad befriending the old horse, and loving him for pure pity's sake, in the sweet childish way we so soon forget.

Posy clapped her hands, mamma smiled, with a bright look at her boy, while Mr. White threw over his arm the halter, with which he was about to lead Major to his doom, and hastened to say, —

"I don't want to hurt the poor critter, ma'am, but he's no mortal use, and folks complain of his being in the way; so I thought the kindest thing was to put him out of his misery."

"Does he suffer, do you think? for if so, it would be no kindness to keep him alive," said mamma.

"Well, no, I don't suppose he suffers except for food and a little care; but if he can't have 'em, it will go hard with him," answered Mr. White, wondering if the old fellow had any work in him still.

"He never should have been left in this forlorn way. Those who had had his youth and strength should have cared for him in his age;" and Mrs. West looked indignant.

"So they should, ma'am; but Miller was a mean man, and when he moved, he just left the old horse to live or die, though he told me, himself, that Major had served him well, for nigh on to twenty years. What do you calculate to do about it, ma'am?" asked Mr. White, in a hurry to be off.

"I 'll show you, sir. Ned, let down the bars, and lead old Major in. That shall be his home while he lives, for so faithful a servant has earned his rest, and he shall have it."

Something in the ring of mamma's voice and the gesture of her hand made Ned's eyes kindle, and Mr. White walk away, saying, affably, —

"All right, ma'am; I haven't a word to say against it."

But somehow Mr. White's big barn did not look as handsome to him as usual when he remembered that his neighbor, who had no barn at all, had taken in the friendless horse.

It was difficult to make Major enter the field; for he had been turned out of so many, driven away from so many lawns, and even begrudged the scanty pickings of the roadside, that he could not understand the invitation given him to enter and take possession of a great, green field, with apple trees for shade, and a brook babbling through the middle of it.

When at last he ventured over the bars, it was both sad and funny to see how hard he tried to enjoy himself and express his delight.

First, he sniffed the air, then he nibbled the sweet grass, took a long look about him, and astonished the children by lying down with a groan, and trying to roll. He could not do it, however, so lay still with his head stretched out, gently flapping his tail as if to say, —

"It's all right, my dears. I'm not very strong, and joy upsets me; but I'm quite comfortable, bless you!"

"Isn't it nice to see him, all safe and happy,

mamma?" sighed Posy, folding her hands in childish satisfaction, while Ned sat down beside *his* horse, and began to take the burrs out of his mane.

"Very nice, only don't kill him with kindness, and be careful not to get hurt," answered mamma, as she went back to her work, feeling as if she had bought an elephant, and didn't know what to do with him.

Later in the day a sudden shower came up, and mamma looked about to be sure her little people were under cover, for they played out all day long, if possible. No chickens could the maternal hen find to gather under her wings, and so went clucking anxiously about till Sally, the cook, said, with a laugh, —

"Ned 's down in the pastur', mum, holding an umberella over that old horse, and he 's got a waterproof on him, too. Calvin see it, and 'most died a-laughing."

Mamma laughed too, but asked if Ned had on his rubber boots and coat.

"Yes, mum, I see him start all in his wet-weather rig, but I never mistrusted what the dear was up to till Calvin told me. Posy wanted to go, but I wouldn't let her, so she went to the upper window, where she can see the critter under his umberella."

Mamma went up to find her little girl surveying the droll prospect with solemn satisfaction; for there in the field, under the apple tree, stood Major, blanketed with the old waterproof, while his new master held an umbrella over his aged head with a patient devotion that would have endeared him to the heart of good Mr. Bergh.

Fortunately the shower was soon over, and Ned came in to dry himself, quite unconscious of any thing funny in his proceedings. Mamma kept perfectly sober while she proposed to build a rough shed for Major out of some boards on the place. Ned was full of interest at once; and with some help from Calvin, the corner under the apple tree was so sheltered that there would be no need of the umbrella hereafter.

So Major lived in clover, and was a happy horse; for Cockletop, the lame chicken, and Bobtail, the cat, welcomed him to their refuge, and soon became fast friends. Cockle chased grasshoppers or pecked about him with meditative clucks as he fed; while Bob rubbed against his legs, slept in his shed, and nibbled catnip socially as often as his constitution needed it.

But Major loved the children best, and they took good care of him, though some of their kind attentions might have proved fatal if the wise old beast had not been more prudent than they. It was pleasant to see him watch for them, with ears cocked at the first sound of the little voices, his dim eyes brightening at sight of the round faces peeping over the wall, and feeble limbs stirred into sudden activity by the beckoning of a childish hand.

The neighbors laughed at Ned, yet liked him all the better for the lesson in kindness he had taught them; and a time came when even Mr. White showed his respect for old Major.

All that summer Neddy's horse took his rest in the green meadow, but it was evident that he was failing fast, and that his "good time" came too late. Mamma prepared the children for the end as well as she could, and would have spared them the sorrow of parting by having Major killed quietly, if Ned had not begged so hard to let his horse die naturally; for age was the only disease, and Major seemed to suffer little pain, though he daily grew more weak, and lame, and blind.

One morning when the children went to carry him a soft, warm mash for breakfast, they found him dead; not in the shed, where they had left him warmly covered, but at the low place in the wall where they always got over to visit him.

There he lay, with head outstretched, as if his last desire had been to get as near them as possible, his last breath spent in thanking them. They liked to think that he crept there to say good by, and took great comfort in the memory of all they had done for him.

They cried over him tenderly, even while they agreed that it was better for him to die; and then they covered him with green boughs, after Ned had smoothed his coat for the last time, and Posy cut a lock from his mane to make mourning rings of.

Calvin said he would attend to the funeral, and went off to dig the grave in a lonely place behind the sand-bank. Ned declared that he could not have his horse dragged away and tumbled into a hole, but must see him buried in a proper manner; and mamma, with the utmost kindness, said she would provide all that was needed.

The hour was set at four in the afternoon, and the two little mourners, provided with large handkerchiefs, Ned, with a black bow on his arm, and Posy in a crape veil, went to drop a last tear over their departed friend.

At the appointed time Calvin appeared, followed by Mr. White, with a drag drawn by black Bill. This delicate attention touched Neddy; for it might have been bay Kitty, and that would have marred the solemnity of the scene.

As the funeral train passed the house on its way down the lane, mamma, with another crape veil on, came out and joined the procession, so full of sympathy that the children felt deeply grateful.

The October woods were gay with red and yellow leaves, that rustled softly as they went through the wood; and when they came to the grave, Ned thanked Calvin for choosing such a pretty place. A pine sighed overhead, late asters waved beside it, and poor Major's last bed was made soft with hemlock boughs.

When he was laid in it, mamma bade them leave the old waterproof that had served for a pall still about him, and then they showered in bright leaves till nothing was visible but a glimpse of the dear white tail.

The earth was thrown in, green sods heaped over it, and then the men departed, feeling that the mourners would like to linger a little while.

As he left, Mr. White said, with the same gravity which he had preserved all through the scene, —

"You are welcome to the use of the team and my time, ma'am. I don't wish any pay for 'em; in fact, I should feel more comfortable to do this job for old Major quite free and hearty."

Mamma thanked him, and when he was gone, Ned proposed that they should sing a hymn, and Posy added, "They always sing, 'Sister, thou art mild and lovely' at funerals, you know."

Mamma with difficulty kept sober at this idea but suggested the song about "Good old Charlie," as more appropriate. So it was sung with great feeling, and then Posy said, as she "wiped her weeping eyes," —

"Now, Ned, show mamma our eppytap."

"She means eppytarf," explained Ned, with a superior air, as he produced a board, on which he had printed with India ink the following words, —

"Here lies dear old Major. He was a good horse when he was young. But people were not kind to him when he was old. We made him as happy as we could. He loved us, and we mourn for him. Amen."

Ned's knowledge of epitaphs was very slight, so he asked mamma if this one would do; and she answered warmly, —

"It is a very good one; for it has what many lack, — the merit of being true. Put it up, dear, and I'll make a wreath to hang on the gravestone."

Much gratified, Ned planted the board at the head of the grave, Posy gathered the brightest leaves, and mamma made a lovely garland in which to frame the "eppytap."

Then they left old Major to his rest, feeling sure that somewhere there must be a lower heaven for the souls of brave and faithful animals when their unrewarded work is done.

Many children went to see that lonely grave, but not one of them disturbed a leaf, or laughed at the little epitaph that preached them a sermon from the text, —

"Blessed are the merciful."

VI.

WHAT THE GIRLS DID.

"I'M so disappointed that I can't go; but papa says he can't afford it this summer. You know we lost a good deal by the great fire, so we must all give up something;" and Nelly gave a sigh, as if her sacrifice was not an easy one.

"I'm sorry, too, for I depend on hearing all about your adventures every summer. It is almost as good as going myself. What a pity Newport is such an expensive place," answered Kitty Fisher, Nelly's bosom friend.

"I dare say papa could manage to let me go for a week or so; but my outfit would cost so much I dare not ask him. One must dress there, you know, and I haven't had a new thing this summer," said Nelly.

"I'm sure your old things as you call them, are nice enough for any place. I should think I was made, if I had such a lovely wardrobe;" and Kitty's eye roved round the pretty room where several gowns and hats were strewn as if for a survey.

"Ah, my dear, you don't know how quickly fashionable women spy out make-shifts, and despise you for them. All the girls I should meet at Newport would remember those clothes and I shouldn't enjoy myself a bit. No, I must stay at home, or slip away to Aunt Becky's, up in New Hampshire, where no one minds your clothes, and the plainer they are the better. It is as dull as tombs up there, and I long for the sea, so it seems as if I *could'nt* give up my trip."

"Why not go to a cheaper place?" asked Kitty, adding, with sudden excitement, "Now look here! This is just the thing, and I can go too, so you won't be lonely.

"Mary Nelson wrote me the other day, begging I'd come down to Oceana, and stay with her. It's a nice, quiet place, with a beach all to ourselves, light-house, rocks, fishing, boats, and all sorts of agreeable things. Not a bit fashionable, and every one wears old clothes and enjoys him or her self in a sensible way."

"What's board there?"

"Ten a week, with bath-house, boats, and an old carriage thrown in."

"Who is there?"

"Several teachers resting, a family or two of children, and a lot of boys camping out on the Point."

"And old clothes really will do?"

"Mary says she lives in her boating-dress, and went to an evening party in a white morning-gown. I'd quite decided to go and have a nice free time, after you were off; but now you come with me, and for once see what fun we poor folks can have without any fuss or feathers."

"I will. Papa wants me to go somewhere, and will not think my expenses down there are extravagant. I'll pack to-day, and to-morrow we will be off."

Next day they *were* off, to be heartily welcomed by Mary, and speedily made at home by Marm Wolsey, as the old lady who kept the house was called. It was a delightfully quiet, pleasant place, with big rooms plainly furnished, but clean and full of fresh sea breezes day and night. Being founded on a rock, the boats were moored almost at the door, the bath-house was close by, on a smooth beach, and the lighthouse twinkled cheerfully, through fog or moonlight, just over the Point.

Such pleasant times as the girls had; taking early

dips in the sea, lying in hammocks on the airy piazza through the hot hours, rowing, fishing, scrambling over the rocks, or sitting in shady nooks, working and reading.

No one thought of clothes; and when Nelly timidly put on a delicate silk one day, she was told finery was not allowed, and a merry resolution was passed that no one should "dress up" under penalty of a fine. So flannel boating suits were all the fashion; and Miss Phelps would have rejoiced at the sight of half-a-dozen rosy-faced girls skipping about the rocks in a costume as simple and sensible as the one she recommends.

Of course the campers on the Point soon discovered the mermaids in the Cove, and, by a series of those remarkable accidents which usually occur at such times, got acquainted without much ceremony.

Then the fun increased amazingly, and the old house saw gay doings; for the lads had bonfires, concerts by moonlight on the rocks, and picnics in every available cove, grove, and sea-weedy nook the place could boast.

The mothers of the flocks of riotous children were matrons to the girls; and the shy teachers came out amazingly when they found that the three friends were not fashionable city ladies, but lively girls, bent on having an agreeable and sociable time.

Nelly particularly enjoyed all this, and daily wondered why she felt so much better than at Newport, forgetting that there her time was spent in dressing by day, and dancing in hot rooms half the night, with no exercise but a drive or a genteel sail, with some one to do the rowing for her.

"It is the air and the quiet, I fancy," she said one day, when a month had nearly gone. "I'm getting so brown papa won't know me, and so fat I have to let out all my things. I do believe I've grown several inches across the shoulders with all this rowing and tramping about in a loose suit."

"Just so much health laid up for next winter. I wish I could afford to bring down a dozen pale girls every season, and let them do what you have been doing for a month or two. Poor girls, I mean, who lose their health by hard work, not by harmful play," said Mary, who knew something about the dark side of life, having been a governess for years, with little brothers and sisters to care for, and an invalid mother.

"It is so cheap here I should think most any one could afford to come," said Nelly, feeling a virtuous satisfaction in the thought of the money she had saved by this economical trip.

"Ah, what seems cheap to you would be far beyond the means of many a poor girl who only makes three or four dollars a week. I've often wondered why rich people don't do little things of that sort more. It must be so pleasant to give health and happiness at such small cost to themselves."

"If papa were as well off as he was before the fire, I *could* do something of that sort, and I'd like to; but now I can do nothing," and Nelly felt rather uncomfortable at the memory of the seventeen easy years she had passed without ever thinking of such things.

"Girls, I've got an idea, and you must give me your advice at once," cried Kitty, bouncing in with her hat half off and her eyes full of fun.

"Tell on. What is it?" asked Nelly, ready for any thing.

"Well, you know the boys have been very polite to us in many ways; they break camp in two days, and we ought to give them a farewell of some sort, to show that we are grateful for their civility. Don't you think so?"

"Of course! What shall we do?"

"We have had picnics and water parties, and sings and dances in our parlor, so we *must* get up something new."

"Have a masquerade; it's such fun to fix up dresses," said Nelly, who rather longed to show some of her neglected splendor.

"We might borrow the old barn, to have a grand time. There's no hay in it, so we could light it up splendidly," added Kitty, seizing upon the idea with delight.

"How about supper?" asked prudent Mary, remembering the appetites of a dozen hearty lads sharpened by sea air and exercise.

"I'll pay for the supper. I've saved so much by my cheap trip, I can spare twenty dollars as well as not," cried Nelly, bound to have the thing done handsomely if at all.

"Bless you, child, it needn't cost half that! Don't go and be extravagant, for we can have cake of Marm Wolsey, and make lemonade ourselves; it won't cost much, and the boys will be just as well off as if we had a grand spread."

"You let me manage that part of the affair. I have ordered suppers at home, and I know what is proper. I will go up to town by the first boat to-morrow, and be back in time to help about dresses, and trimming up the barn. Marm will lend us sheets, and with green boughs, flowers, and candles, we can make a lovely room for our little party. I'll bring down some colored candles, and get some old-fashioned dresses at home, and do any errands for you."

Here Nelly stopped for breath, and the others fell to discussing what they would "go as." Their fellow-boarders were taken into the secret, and in an hour Marm Wolsey's whole establishment was in a ferment. Notes of invitation were dispatched; and replies on birch-bark came pouring in with most agreeable promptitude.

The campers accepted to a man, and were soon seen ravaging the little town for red flannel and fisherman's toggery, or shouting with laughter in their tents as they fabricated horse-hair beards, Indian wampum and Roman armor.

Next morning Nelly departed, charged with sundry very important commissions, and the rest fell to work decorating the barn and overhauling their wardrobes, while good-natured Marm "het the big oven" and made cake till the air smelt as if a gale from the Spice Islands had blown over the Point.

At four, the boat came in; but no one saw Nelly

arrive, for the whole flock had gone over the rocks to get hemlock boughs in the grove.

When Mary and Kitty returned, they ran to the big room where they held their confabulations, and there found Nelly looking over a bundle of old brocades. Something odd in her face and manner made them both say at once, —

"What 's the matter? Has any thing gone wrong?"

"I 'm afraid you will think so, when I tell you that I have ordered no supper, got no pretty candles or flowers, and only spent two dollars of my money," said Nelly, looking both amused and anxious.

"Lost your purse?" cried Kitty.

"No."

"Thought better of it, like a wise child," said Mary.

"I brought something down that you didn't ask for, and may be sorry to have; but I couldn't help it. Look out there and see if that isn't better than bon-bons or finery."

Nelly pointed to a rock not far from the window, and both her friends stared in surprise; for all they saw was a strange girl sitting there, gazing out over the sea with an expression of wordless delight in her tired, white face and hungry eyes.

"Who is it?" whispered Mary.

"My little seamstress," answered Nelly. "I went to get her to fix my dress, and found her looking so pale and used up my heart ached. All the while she was fitting me, and I was telling her about our fun down here, she kept saying with a little gasp as if for fresh air, —

"'How beautiful it must be, Miss Nelly! I'm so glad you are enjoying so much and look so well.'

"Then what you once said, Mary, came into my head, and my money burnt in my pocket till I broke out all of a sudden, saying, —

"'Wouldn't you like to go down with me for a week and get rested and freshened up a little, Jane?'

"Girls, if I had asked her to go straight to heaven, or do any lovely thing, she could not have looked more amazed, delighted, and touched.

"'O, Miss Nelly, you are too good. I'm afraid I ought not to leave work. It seems almost too splendid to believe.'

"I wouldn't hear a word, for my heart was set on doing it when I saw how she longed to go. So I said she could help us with our dresses, and I must have her come on that account if no other.

"Then she said she had nothing fit to wear, and I was *so* glad to be able to tell her that none of us wore nice clothes, and hers were quite fit. I just made her put on her bonnet, brought her away in the twinkling of an eye, and there she is enjoying rest, fresh air, sunshine and her first view of the sea."

"Nelly, you are an angel!" and Kitty hugged her on the spot, while Mary beamed at her with tears in her eyes, as she said, quietly, —

"I did not think my little sermon would be so soon and beautifully taken to heart. The sight of that poor child, sitting there so happy, is better than the most splendid supper you could have ordered. I shall always love and honor you for this, dear."

Nelly's face was a pretty mixture of smiles and tears, as her friends kissed and praised her. Then she said, brightly, —

"Now we will have nothing but our cake and lemonade, and make up in good spirits for the supper we have lost. Flowers will do for favors, and tallow candles will help the moon light up our 'hall.' See my Bo-Peep dress; and here are lots of things for you. To-morrow Jane will help us, and we will be splendiferous."

Three happy faces bent over the old brocades,

three busy tongues chattered gaily of trains and flounces, and three pairs of friendly eyes peeped often at the quiet figure on the rocks, finding greater satisfaction in that sweet little tableau than in any they could plan.

Merry times they had next day, for Jane's skilful fingers worked wonders, and gratitude inspired her with all manner of brilliant ideas. She was introduced as a friend; any deficiencies in her wardrobe were quietly supplied by Nelly, and she proved herself an invaluable ally, enjoying every minute of the precious time.

Nothing could have been prettier in its way than the old barn, draped with sails and sheets, with flags and pennons from the boats, great peonies and green boughs for decorations. Candles and lanterns twinkled their best, and the great doors at both ends stood wide open, letting in floods of moonlight, fresh air and lovely glimpses of the sea.

The neighbors all came to "peek," and the hearty laughter of the big brown fishermen clustered round the door was good to hear, as the comical, quaint, or charming figures entered the room. Tow-headed children roosted on the beams, women in calico gowns sat staring in the stalls, while babies slept placidly in the hay-racks, and one meek cow surveyed the scene with astonished eyes.

Powhattan, St. George, Brother Jonathan, Capt. Cuttle, Garibaldi and other noble beings came from the camp, to find Bo-Peep in a ravishing little costume, with a Quakeress, Sairey Gamp, Dolly Varden and a host of other delightful ladies ready to receive them.

What happy hours followed, with the promenades, and plays, and homely yet delightful surroundings. The barn was so cool, so spacious, and every thing was so free and simple, that every one "went in and enjoyed himself like a man," as Capt. Kyd gracefully remarked to Mary Nelson, who was capitally and cheaply got up as the Press, dressed in newspapers, with a little telegraph, posts, wires and all, on her head.

Fruit, cake and lemonade was all the feast, spread on the big rock in front of the barn, and no one complained; for moonlight, youth and happy hearts lent their magic to the scene.

"Never had such a good time in my life," was the general verdict when the party broke up at eleven, and the gallant guests departed, to return the compliment by a charming serenade an hour later.

"Now that just puts the last touch to it. So romantic and delicious!" sighed Nelly, listening luxuriously to the melodious strains of that college favorite, "Juanita."

"It 's all like a beautiful dream to me," sighed Jane, who was peeping through the blinds with the other pretty white ghosts, and enjoying the whole thing to her heart's core.

Kitty threw out some flowers, and when each youth had stuck a relic in his button-hole, the sailor hats disappeared, leaving only the musical assurance that "Her bright smile haunts me still," to echo over the rocks and die away in the lapping of the tide upon the shore.

A quiet week followed, and the girls spent it teaching Jane to row and swim, taking her to drive in the old wagon, and making her "have a good time."

She was so blissfully happy and improved so much that Nelly had serious thoughts of applying to her father for more money, so that Jane might stay longer. But though she said not a word about her little charity, the truth crept out, and several of the ladies quietly made up a handsome sum for Jane.

They gave it to Nelly, asking her to use it and say nothing of them, lest it should annoy the little seamstress. So Nelly, when her own time was up, had the pleasure of telling Jane she was to stay some weeks longer, and of slipping into her hand the means so kindly provided for her.

She had no words in which to thank these friends, but her happy face did it as she bade them good-by, when they left her smiling, with wet eyes, among the roses in the lane.

"Our visit has been a success, though it wasn't Newport, hey, Nelly?" said Kitty, as they rumbled away in the big omnibus.

"Oh, yes! I've had a lovely time, and mean to come next summer and bring another Jane, to go halves with me; it gives such a relish to one's fun somehow," answered Nelly, contentedly tying on her last year's hat.

"Old clothes, wholesome pleasures and a charitable deed are all the magic that has made your month so happy and so helpful," said Mary, putting an affectionate arm about the shoulders in the now faded jacket.

"And good friends; don't forget to add that," answered Nelly, with a grateful kiss.

VII.

LITTLE NEIGHBORS.

TWITTER THE FIRST.

"MAMMA, I do wish I had a nice, new play. Can't you make me one?" said Bertie, pensively surveying the soles of his shoes, as he lay flat on his back with his heels in the air.

"No, dear, I couldn't possibly stop now, for I must write my letters, or they won't be in time, and papa will be disappointed."

"Then I wish I had somebody to play with me! A jolly little chap who would amuse me and make me laugh," continued Bertie, and, dropping his legs, he lay for a moment, looking as if he really did need a playmate very much.

"Tweet! tweet!" said a little voice, in such a brisk tone that the boy stared about him eager to see who spoke.

One pane of the long window that opened on the balcony was fixed like a door, so that the room might be ventilated. This pane stood open, and perched upon its threshold was a sparrow peering in with an inquisitive air, and a bold "Tweet! tweet!" as if he said, —

"Here's a little friend all ready to play with you."

"Oh, mamma, see the cunning bird! He wants to come in! Don't stir, and may be he'll hop down and eat the crumbs of my luncheon on the table. It's Cocky Twitters; I know him by his tail, with only two feathers in it, and his twinkling eye, and his little fat body," cried Bertie, lying as still as a statue, and looking with delight at the new-comer.

You see Bertie lived near a square where many English sparrows had their homes, and all winter the kind child fed his little neighbors. Day after day he strewed crumbs in the balcony, and day after day the birds came to peck them gratefully, or to fly away with the big bits to their nests. So they learned to know and love and trust each other, and the passers-by often saw a pretty sight up in the sunny balcony where the delicate boy stood with his feathered friends about him; some at his feet, some on his shoulders, some boldly stealing crumbs from his basket, and the more timid hopping about on the wide balustrade, catching such stray mouthfuls as reached them.

Bertie was fond of his birds, and had names for

some of them, but his favorite was Cocky Twitters, a bold, saucy, droll fellow, who was always whisking about as if he had every thing in the bird-world to attend to. He fought like a little game-cock if any other sparrow troubled him, but he was good to the weak and timid ones, and never failed to carry a nice crumb or two to his old papa, who had something the matter with his wing, and seldom went far from the little brown house stuck like a wasp's nest on one of the trees.

Cocky had often thought about coming in to call, but never had found the courage to really do it, so Bertie was enchanted when, after a good deal of tweeting, much perking up of his smooth head, and many a sidelong twinkle of his little black eye, Cocky actually hopped down upon the table.

Mamma sat motionless, smiling at her little guest, and Bertie hardly dared to wink as he watched his pet's pranks.

Cocky had evidently made up his mind to have a right good time, and see, taste, examine, and enjoy all he found in this new world. So he paraded about the table, ate a bit of cake, pecked at an apple, and drank prettily out of Bertie's silver mug; then he wiped his bill quite properly, took a look at the books, peeped into the inkstand, draggled his tail in the gum-pot, examined mamma's work-basket, and took a sniff at the flowers. After that he strolled over the carpet with such a funny swagger of his thin legs, such an important roll of his fat, little body, and such an impudent cock of his head, that Bertie burst out laughing, which made Cocky flit away to the top of the clock, where he sat and twittered as if he was laughing too.

"I wish I could keep him a few days, he is *so* jolly! Couldn't I put him in Dickey's cage, and feed and be good to him, mamma?"

"He would never trust you again if you did."

"But I should 'splain it to him, and tell him it was only a visit."

"He wouldn't like it, and I think you will enjoy him more when he makes visits of his own accord. He would be the maddest little bird that ever flew if you shut him up; but leave him free, and every day it will be a pleasure to open the pane and see him come in confidingly. He is tired of this warm room already, and trying to get out. Show him the way, and let him go."

"I'll have one good feel of him anyhow, but I won't hurt him," said Bertie, yielding the point, but bound to get a little fun out of his fat friend before he went.

So he danced about after Cocky, who was so bewildered he could not find his own little door, and bounced against all the wrong panes till he was dizzy, and fell down in a corner. Then Bertie softly grabbed him and though he pecked fiercely, Bertie got a "good feel" of the soft, warm mite. Then he let him go, and Cocky sat on the balustrade and chirped till all his friends came to see what the fuss was about.

"Oh, I do wish I could understand what they say. He's telling them all about his visit, and they look so cunning, sitting round listening and asking questions. You know French and German; don't you know bird-talk too, mamma?" asked Bertie, turning round, after he had stood with his nose against the glass till it was as cold as a little icicle.

"No, dear, I am sorry to say I don't."

"I thought mammas knew every thing," said Bertie, in a disappointed tone.

"They ought to if they expect to answer all the questions their children ask them," answered mamma, with a sigh, for Bertie had an inquiring mind and often puzzled his parents sorely.

"I suppose you haven't got time to learn it?" was the next remark.

"Decidedly not. But *you* have, so you'd better begin at once, and let me go on with my work."

"I don't know how to begin."

"You must ask some wiser person than I am about that," answered mamma, scratching away at a great rate.

"I know what I'll do!" said Bertie, after meditating deeply for a few minutes; and, putting on his cap and coat, he went out upon the balcony.

Mamma thought he had gone to consult Cocky, and forgot all about him for a time. But Bertie had another plan in his head, and went resolutely up to one of the windows of the next house. It opened on the same balcony, and only a low bar separated the houses, so Bertie often promenaded up and down the whole length, and more than once had peeped under the half-drawn curtain at the gray-headed gentleman who always seemed to be too busy with his books to see his little neighbor.

Bertie had heard Professor Parpatharges Patterson called a very learned man, who could read seven languages, so he thought he would call and inquire if bird language was among the seven. He peeped first, and there was Mr. P. reading away with his big spectacles on, and some dreadfully wise old book held close to his nose. As he did not look up, Bertie tapped softly, but Mr. P. did not hear. Then this resolute young person pushed up the window, walked coolly in, and stood close to the student's side. But Mr. P. did not see him till the remarkable appearance of a small blue mitten right in the middle of Plato's Republic, caused the Professor to start and stare at it with such a funny expression of bewilderment that Bertie could not help laughing.

The blithe sound seemed to wake the man out of a dream, for, falling back in his chair, he sat blinking at the child like a surprised owl.

"Please, sir, I knocked, but you didn't hear, so I came in," said Bertie, with an engaging smile, as he respectfully pulled off his cap and looked up at the big spectacles with bright, confiding eyes.

"What did you wish, boy?" asked the Professor, in a solemn, yet not ungentle, tone.

"I wanted to know if you would tell me how I could learn bird-talk."

"What?" and the man stared at the child harder than ever.

"Perhaps I'd better sit down and 'splain all about

it," remarked Bertie, feeling that the subject was too important to be hastily discussed.

"Take a seat, boy;" and the Professor waved his hand vaguely, as if he did not know much about any chair but his own old one, with the stuffing bursting out, and ink spots everywhere.

As all the chairs had books and papers piled up in them, Bertie, with great presence of mind, sat down upon an immense dictionary that lay near by, and with a hand on either knee, thus briefly explained himself:

"My mamma said that you were very wise, and could read seven langwitches, so I thought you would please tell me what Cocky Twitters says."

"Is Twitters a bird or a boy?" asked the Professor, as if bewildered by what seemed a very simple affair to innocent Bertie.

At this question, the boy burst forth into an eager recital of his acquaintance with the sparrows, giving a little bounce on the fat dictionary now and then when he got excited, while his rosy face shone with an eagerness that was irresistible.

The Professor listened as if to a language which he had almost forgotten, while the ghost of a smile began to flicker over his lips, and peer out from behind his glasses, as if somewhere about him there was a heart that tried to welcome the little guest, who came tapping at the long-closed door.

When Bertie ended, out of breath, Mr. P. said, slowly, while he looked about as if to find something he had lost, — "I understand now, but I 'm afraid I 've forgotten all I ever knew about birds, — and boys too," he added, with an odd twinkle of the glasses.

"Couldn't you *reccomember* if you tried hard, sir?"

"I don't think I could."

Bertie gave a great sigh, and cast a reproachful glance upon the Professor, which said as plainly as words, "You must have been a *very* idle man to live among books till you are gray, and not know a simple thing like this."

I think Mr. P. understood that look, and felt ashamed of his sad ignorance; for he rose up and went walking about the room, poking into corners and peering up at the books that lined the walls, till he found a large volume, and brought it to Bertie, who still sat despondently upon the dictionary.

"Perhaps this will help us. It tells much about birds, and the tales are all true."

Bertie caught the book in his arms, laid it open on his knees, and with one delighted "Oh!" at the first peep, became entirely absorbed in the gay pictures. With an air of relief, the Professor retired to his chair, and sat watching him very much as he had watched Cocky Twitters. A pretty little picture he made; for a ray of sunshine crept in to shine on his bright head like a playmate come to find him; his downy brows were knit, and his rosy mouth pursed up at times with the mingled exertions of mind and body, for the book was both beautiful and heavy. His eyes feasted on the pages; and now and then he laughed out with delight, as he found a bird he knew, or gave a satisfied nod, and trotted his foot to express his satisfaction at some unusually splendid one. Once he tried to cross his tired legs, but they were too short, and the book went down with a bang that made him glance at his host in alarm.

But while he studied Audubon's birds, the Professor had studied mamma's boy, and found he *could* "reccomember" some of the traits belonging to *that* species of wild-fowl. As he looked, the smile had been playing hide-and-go-seek among his wrinkles, getting less ghostly every minute, and when the book fell, it came boldly out and sat upon his face so pleasantly, that Bertie ceased to be afraid.

"Put it on the table, boy," said Mr. P., beckoning with an inky finger.

Bertie lugged his treasure thither, and leaning both elbows on it, began to brood again. It really did seem as if the Professor wanted to have a good "feel" of the boy as the boy did of Cocky, for presently the inky finger softly stroked the yellow head, then touched the round, red cheek, and put a little curl back behind the ear. Then the spectacles took a long look all over the little figure, from the striped stockings to the fur collar on the small coat, and something about it, a certain chubbiness of outline and softness of exterior perhaps, seemed to be so attractive, that, all of a sudden, two large hands hovered over Bertie, gently clutched him, and set him on the Professor's knee.

If Mr. P. felt any doubts as to how his guest would take this liberty, they were speedily set at rest, for Bertie only gave one wiggle to settle himself, and, turning a page, said affably, —

"Now, tell me all about 'em."

And Professor Parpatharges Patterson actually

did tell him story after story out of that charming book, till the sound of a bell made the truant jump down in a great hurry, saying, —

"Mamma wants me, and I must go, but I'll come again soon, and may be, if we study hard, we shall learn bird-talk after all."

Mr. P. shook his head; but Bertie would not give up yet, and added encouragingly, —

"Mamma says people are never too old to learn, and papa says Latin makes all the other langwitches easy; I see lots of Latin books, and you read 'em, so I'm sure, if you listen to my sparrows, when I feed 'em, you *can* understand some of their talk."

"I'll try, and let you know how I get on," said Mr. P., laughing as if he didn't know how very well, but couldn't help making the attempt.

"I'm very much obliged to you, sir, and I shall be glad to pay you for your trouble. I've got two dollars in my tin bank, and I'll smash it, and get 'em out, if that will be enough," said Bertie, suddenly remembering to have heard that Mr. P. was not rich.

"No, boy, I don't want your pennies, you shall pay in some other way, if I succeed," answered the Professor, with a touched sort of look about the spectacles.

"I've had a very nice time. Good day, sir," and Bertie held out his hand, as he made his best bow.

"Good day, boy. Come again."

I think there must have been some magic about that blue mitten, or the warm little hand inside, for, as he held it quite buried up in his own big one, Mr. P. suddenly stooped down, and said, in a queer, bashful sort of tone, —

"Suppose you pay with kisses, if you have any to spare."

"I've got hundreds; I always keep 'em ready, because mamma needs so many," and Bertie held up his rosy mouth, as if this sort of coin best suited the treasury of a loving heart.

Considering that the Professor had not kissed any one for twenty years at least, he did it very well, and, when Bertie was gone, stood looking down at the corpulent old dictionary, as if he still saw a bright-eyed little figure sitting on it, and considered that a great improvement upon the dust that usually lay there.

TWITTER THE SECOND.

Mamma was right; for Cocky, finding himself well treated at his first visit, called again, and being feasted on sugar, fruit, and cake, and allowed to go when he liked, was entirely won. From that time he was the friend of the family, and called as regularly as the postman. He knew his own little door, and if it was shut he tapped with his bill till some one opened it, when he came bustling in, chirping a gay "How are you?" and waggling his ragged tail in the most friendly manner. Weather made no difference to him; in fact rainy days were his favorite times for calling. His little coat was waterproof, he needed no umbrella, and often came hopping in, with snow-flakes on his back, as jolly as you please.

I don't know what Bertie would have done without this sociable little neighbor, for it was a stormy winter and he could not go out much; other children were at school; even mamma's inventive powers gave out sometimes, and toys grew tiresome. But Cocky never did, and such games as the two had together it would have done your heart good to see, for the boy was so gentle that the bird soon grew very tame and learned to love and trust with the sweetest confidence. A jollier sparrow never hopped; and after a good lunch with Bertie, both drinking out of one mug, both pecking at the same apple, and sharing the same cake, Cocky was ready for play. He would hide somewhere and Bertie would hunt for him, guided now and then by a faint "Tweet" till the little gray bunch was found in some sly nook and came bouncing out with a whisk and a chirp.

When Bertie sat at lessons, Cocky would roost on his shoulder, hop over the open page with his head on one side as if reading it, peer into the inkstand inquisitively, or settle himself among the flowers that stood in the middle of the table, like a little teacher ready to hear the lessons when they were learned.

And sometimes when Bertie lay asleep, tired with books or play, Cocky would circle round him with soft flight, and perch on his pillow, waiting silently till his playmate woke, "like an angel guarding the dear in his sleep," as old nurse said, watching the pretty sight.

Professor Parpatharges Patterson was right also; for he apparently did try to understand "bird-talk," and did succeed; for a few days after Bertie's call a letter came flying in at the open pane just at twilight, very much as if Cocky had brought it himself. It was written on robin's-egg-colored paper, and bore the title, "Life and Adventures of Cocky Twitters, Esq."

Mamma began to laugh as she glanced over it, and Bertie screamed with delight when a funny sketch appeared of an egg with a very small but brisk little bird hopping out of it without a feather on him. It was very funny, and when mamma read Cocky's thoughts and feelings on first beholding the world, it was so droll, and Bertie was so tickled, that he rolled on the floor and kicked up his heels.

Mr. P. must have tried very hard to "reccomember" the accomplishments and gayety of his youth, for the sketch was so good and the first chapter of this bird-book so merry that mamma put it in a little portfolio and showed it to all her friends, for no one ever dreamed that the studious old Professor had it in him to do such a clever thing.

Bertie wanted to rush right in and thank him that very night, but mamma said he had better wait till morning and then play a little joke in return for the Professor's. So next day, when Mr. P. pulled up the curtain of his study window, there hung a lovely posy of flowers and a little card with "Bertie Norton's compliments and thanks" on it.

That pleased the old man; and all that day the roses filled his room with their sweet breath, mutely talking to him of a happy time when his little daughter used to put nosegays on his table, and dance about him like a blooming rose escaped from its stem. For years no one had thought to scatter flowers among the wise books out of which the poor man tried to gather forgetfulness, if not happiness. No one guessed that he had a lonely heart as well as a learned head, and no childish hand had clung to his till the blue mitten rested there, unconsciously leading him from his sad solitude to the sweet society of a little neighbor.

Bertie soon called again, and this time Mr. P. heard, saw, and welcomed him at once. A cushion lay on the fat dictionary, the bird-book was all ready, the eyes behind the big spectacles beamed with satisfaction as the boy climbed on his knee, and the inky hands held the chubby guest more eagerly and carefully than the most precious old book ever printed.

After that second call the new friendship flourished wonderfully, and the boy became to the Professor what Cocky was to Bertie, a merry, innocent visitor, whose pretty plays and pranks cheered the dull days, whose love and confidence warmed his heart, whose presence grew more and more precious since its unconscious power made sunshine for the lonely man.

Such good times as they had! Such nice chats and stories, such laughs at very small jokes, such plans for summer, such fun feeding the sparrows, who soon learned to come to both windows fearlessly, and such splendid chapters as were added to "C. Twitter's Life and Adventures," with designs that half killed mamma with laughing.

The people in the house were much amused with the change in the Professor, and for a time could not understand what was going on up in that once quiet room. For the sound of little feet trotting about was heard, also a cheery child's voice, and now and then a loud bang as if a pile of books had tumbled down, followed by shouts of merriment, for Mr. P. could laugh capitally after a little practice.

Stout Mrs. Bouncer, the landlady, went up one day to see what was going on, and was so surprised at the spectacle that met her eyes she could hardly believe her senses.

In the middle of the room was a house built of the

precious books which the maid had been forbidden to touch, and in the middle of this barricade sat Bertie, reading "Æsop's Fables" aloud. The table which used to be filled with Greek and Hebrew volumes, learned treatises, and intricate problems was now bestrewn with gay pictures, and Mr. P., with his spectacles pushed back, his cuffs turned up, and a towel tied round him, was busily pasting these brilliant designs into a scrap-book bound in parchment and ornamented with brass clasps.

The Professor evidently had made up his mind that the faded pages were much improved by the gay pictures, and sat smiling over his work as he saw a dead language blossom into flowers, and heard it sing from the throats of golden orioles and soaring larks.

"Well, I never!" said Mrs. Bouncer to herself, and then added aloud, after a long stare, "Do you want any thing sir?"

"Nothing, thank you, ma'am, unless you happen to have a couple of apples in the house. Good, big, red ones, if you please," answered Mr. P., so briskly that she couldn't help laughing, as she said,—

"I'll send 'em right up, sir, and a fresh jumble or so for the little boy."

"Thank you, ma'am, thank you. We fellows have been hard at it for an hour, and we are as hungry as bears; hey, Bertie?"

"I 'm fond of jumbles," was the young student's suggestive reply, as he peeped over the walls with a nod and a smile.

"Bless my heart, what has come to the Professor!" thought Mrs. Bouncer, as she hastened away, while Mr. P. waved his paste brush and Bertie kissed his hand to her.

The neighbors said the same when they saw the two playmates walking out together, as they often did in fine weather. Five old ladies, who sat all day at their different windows watching their neighbors, were so astonished at the sudden appearance of the Professor, hand-in-hand with a yellow-haired little laddie, that they could hardly believe their spectacles. When they saw him drawing Bertie round the square on his sled Racer, they lifted their ten old hands in utter amazement, and when they beheld him actually snowballing, and being snowballed by, that mite of a boy, they really thought the sky must be going to fall.

Mamma heartily enjoyed all this; for through her doctor she had learned much about Mr. P., and both admired and pitied him, and was very glad that Bertie had so wise and kind a playmate. She saw that they did each other good, and in many delicate ways helped the boy to serve, amuse and repay the man who made him so happy.

Cocky also approved of the new friend, and called occasionally to express his views on education. He was very affable, but never allowed Mr. P. to take the same liberties that Bertie did, and after a general survey, would light upon the bald pate of a plaster Homer, whence he watched the boys at play, with deep interest. Mr. P. was immensely flattered by Cocky's visits, and made his "Life" so interesting and droll, that Bertie really believed that the man and bird did it between them.

"I owe a great deal to Mr. Twitters, and I hope I shall discover a way to show my gratitude," said the Professor more than once, and he did, as you will see. It was a very happy winter, in spite of rain and snow, and as spring came on, the three friends had fine times in the park. Bertie fed his birds there now; and they, remembering how he had kept them alive through the bitter weather, seemed to love him more than ever. They flocked round him as soon as he appeared, chirping, fluttering, pecking, and hopping so fearlessly and gayly, that people often came to see the pretty sight, and "Bertie's birds" were one of the lions of the neighborhood.

Cocky was very busy and important about this time. His tail-feathers had grown again, he seemed to have put on a new drab waistcoat, and his head was so sleek that Bertie was sure he used pomade. When he called at the balcony, he often brought another sparrow with him,—a plump, downy bird, with a bright eye, a Quakerish dress, and very gentle manners.

"Mamma says Cocky is going to be married, and that pretty one is his little sweetheart. Won't it be nice? I wonder if he will ask us to the wedding, and where he will live!" said Bertie, standing still in the park, staring up at the nests stuck on the elm boughs, now green with tender leaves and noisy with happy birds.

"I don't think he will ask us, and I very much fear that there won't be room in that brown nest for the old papa and the young folks also," answered Mr. P., staring as hard as Bertie did.

"Then we must ask the mayor to have a new

house put up for Cocky. Don't you think he would if I wrote him a nice letter and showed him your book? He'd see what a brave good bird my Twitters is, and give him a nice house, I'm sure," said Bertie earnestly, for he would believe that Cocky had really done all the fine and funny things recounted in that remarkable book.

"Leave it to me, boy. I will see what can be done about a mansion for Cocky to begin house-keeping in;" and Mr. P. gave a knowing nod, as if he had a new idea.

So Bertie said no more, and, soon after this conversation, went to Plymouth, on a visit with mamma. May-day was coming, and Bertie wanted to hang baskets on the doors of young and old neighbors; chief among the latter his dear Mr. P.

Nowhere in New England do May-flowers grow so large and rosy, or bloom so early and so sweet as in Plymouth, and Bertie gathered a great hamper full of the best, made up in nosegays, garlands, and baskets. Then they came home, and all along the way people sniffed and peeped and smiled at the odorous load which the boy guarded so carefully and rejoiced over so much.

Very early next morning, Bertie and mamma

set out to hang the May-baskets on a dozen doors. The five old ladies each had one, and were immensely pleased at being remembered; for Bertie had discovered that hearts can be young in spite of gray hair, and proposed doing this all himself. Then there was a sick lady who used to look out at the child as he played, with a sad, white face and wistful eyes; two pretty little girls came next, and had raptures in their night-gowns, when the baskets were brought up to them in bed.

Down in a back street was a lame boy who made hockey-sticks; a blind woman who knit the blue mittens, and several children who never had a flower except the dusty dandelions in the park. One can easily imagine how happy these bits of spring made them, and how they welcomed the sweet things with their woody fragrance and rosy faces.

When the last was given, mamma proposed a little walk over the bridge, for it was a lovely day, and she seemed in no haste about breakfast.

Bertie was very hungry before they got back, and was quite ready to go in the back way, directly to the dining-room, where his bread and milk was waiting for him. Right in the middle of breakfast,

Mary, the girl, gave mamma a card, on which was written two words: "All ready!"

Why mamma should laugh when she read it, and why Mary should say, in a whisper, "It's just lovely, ma'am," and then run out of the room giggling, Bertie could not understand.

"Can't I know, mamma?" he asked, feeling sure that some joke or secret was afoot.

"Yes, dear, all in good time. Go now and see if Mr. Patterson has found the May-flowers you hung on his window."

Away went Bertie to the balcony, found the posy gone, and the room empty; so he turned about and was going back, when all of a sudden he saw something that nearly took his breath away with surprise and delight.

Now you must know that the house on the other side of Bertie's jutted out a little, and the niche thus made was covered with a woodbine that climbed up from the grass-plot below. All summer this vine rustled its green leaves above that end of the balcony; in the autumn it hung crimson streamers there, and through the winter the sparrows loved to cuddle down among the twisted stems, sunning their backs in the sheltered corner, and pressing their downy breasts against the warm bricks. Bertie used to hang great shells full of plants there, and called it his garden, but now something even more delightful and ornamental than ivy or flame-colored nasturtiums met his eye.

Up among the budding sprays stood a charming little house, with a wide piazza all round it; a white house, with cunning windows and a tiny porch, where the door stood hospitably open, with the owner's name painted on it.

When Bertie read "C. Twitters," he had to hold on to the railing, lest he should tumble over, so pleased was he with this delightful surprise. As if nothing was wanting to make it quite perfect, Cocky himself came flying up to say "Good morning;" and after a long survey of the new house went to examine it. He walked all round the piazza, sat upon the chimney to see if that was all right, popped his head into the porch, appeared to read the name on the door, and to understand all about it, for with one shrill chirp, he walked in and took possession at once.

Then Bertie danced for joy and called out, "Oh, mamma, come and see! He likes it; he's gone in, and I'm sure he means to live there!"

Mamma came, and so did Mr. P., both pretending to be much amazed at Cocky's daring to build a house so near without asking leave.

But Bertie was not deceived a bit, and hugged them both on the spot, with many thanks for this charming joke, while Cocky sat at his door and twittered, like a grateful, happy little bird, as he was.

That was only the beginning of it; for the interesting things that happened after this May-day were too many to tell. Cocky was married at once, and went to house-keeping in his new villa. Mrs. Twitters evidently liked it extremely, and began to bring in her straw furniture and feather-beds, like a busy little house-wife. Papa Twitters came too; though they had a hard job to get him there, he was so lame with rheumatism. But the vine helped the poor old dear; for after he had got safely across the street, he hopped up the woodbine, little by little, till he got to the porch, and there sat down to rest.

He did not stay long, however, for, like a wise bird, he felt that the young folks would do better alone, and after a nice visit, he returned to the brown nest in the park, where his children called every day and never forgot to take the old papa a crumb of comfort.

Cocky made an excellent husband, and often brought his wife to call on Bertie, who, when the warm days came, sat much in the balcony, always ready for a chat, a game, or a song. All the other birds were chirping gayly, so he joined the chorus; and his favorite was that merry ballad beginning, —

" A little cock-sparrow,
Sat up in a tree,
And whistled, and whistled,
And thus whistled he."

While Bertie and Cocky sang, mamma smiled over her work within, and a gray head often popped out of Mr. P.'s window, as if he loved to listen and to learn still more of the sweet, new language his little neighbors taught him.

VIII.

MARJORIE'S THREE GIFTS.

MARJORIE sat on the door-step, shelling peas, quite unconscious what a pretty picture she made, with the roses peeping at her through the lattice work of the porch, the wind playing hide-and-seek in her curly hair, while the sunshine with its silent magic changed her faded gingham to a golden gown, and shimmered on the bright tin pan as if it were a silver shield. Old Rover lay at her feet, the white kitten purred on her shoulder, and friendly robins hopped about her in the grass, chirping "A happy birthday, Marjorie!"

But the little maid neither saw nor heard, for her eyes were fixed on the green pods, and her thoughts were far away. She was recalling the fairy-tale granny told her last night, and wishing with all her heart that such things happened nowadays. For in this story, as a poor girl like herself sat spinning before the door, a Brownie came by, and gave the child a good-luck penny; then a fairy passed, and left a talisman which would keep her always happy; and last of all, the prince rolled up in his chariot, and took her away to reign with him over a lovely kingdom, as a reward for her many kindnesses to others.

When Marjorie imagined this part of the story, it was impossible to help giving one little sigh, and for a minute she forgot her work, so busy was she thinking what beautiful presents she would give to all the poor children in her realm when *they* had birthdays. Five impatient young peas took this opportunity to escape from the half-open pod in her hand and skip down the steps, to be immediately gobbled up by an audacious robin, who gave thanks in such a shrill chirp that Marjorie woke up, laughed, and fell to work again. She was just finishing, when a voice called out from the lane,—

"Hi, there! come here a minute, child!" and looking up, she saw a little old man in a queer little carriage drawn by a fat little pony.

Running down to the gate, Marjorie dropped a curtsy, saying pleasantly,—

"What did you wish, sir?"

"Just undo that check-rein for me. I am lame, and Jack wants to drink at your brook," answered the old man, nodding at her till his spectacles danced on his nose.

Marjorie was rather afraid of the fat pony, who tossed his head, whisked his tail, and stamped his feet as if he was of a peppery temper. But she liked to be useful, and just then felt as if there were few things she could *not* do if she tried, because it was her birthday. So she proudly let down the rein, and when Jack went splashing into the brook, she stood on the bridge, waiting to check him up again after he had drunk his fill of the clear, cool water.

The old gentleman sat in his place, looking up at the little girl, who was smiling to herself as she watched the blue dragon-flies dance among the ferns, a blackbird tilt on the alder-boughs, and listened to the babble of the brook.

"How old are you, child?" asked the old man, as if he rather envied the rosy creature her youth and health.

"Twelve to-day, sir;" and Marjorie stood up straight and tall, as if mindful of her years.

"Had any presents?" asked the old man, peering up with an odd smile.

"One, sir,—here it is;" and she pulled out of

her pocket a tin savings-bank in the shape of a desirable family mansion, painted red, with a green door and black chimney. Proudly displaying it on the rude railing of the bridge, she added, with a happy face, —

"Granny gave it to me, and all the money in it is going to be mine."

"How much have you got?" asked the old gentleman, who appeared to like to sit there in the middle of the brook, while Jack bathed his feet and leisurely gurgled and sneezed.

"Not a penny yet, but I'm going to earn some," answered Marjorie, patting the little bank with an air of resolution pretty to see.

"How will you do it?" continued the inquisitive old man.

"Oh, I'm going to pick berries and dig dandelions, and weed, and drive cows, and do chores. It is vacation, and I can work all the time, and earn ever so much."

"But vacation is play-time, — how about that?"

"Why, that sort of work *is* play, and I get bits of fun all along. I always have a good swing when I go for the cows, and pick flowers with the dandelions. Weeding isn't so nice, but berrying is very pleasant, and we have good times all together."

"What shall you do with your money when you get it?"

"Oh, lots of things! Buy books and clothes for school, and, if I get a great deal, give some to granny. I'd love to do that, for she takes care of me, and I'd be so proud to help her!"

"Good little lass!" said the old gentleman, as he put his hand in his pocket. "Would you now?" he added, apparently addressing himself to a large frog who sat upon a stone, looking so wise and grandfatherly that it really did seem quite proper to consult him. At all events, he gave his opinion in the most decided manner, for, with a loud croak, he turned an undignified somersault into the brook, splashing up the water at a great rate. "Well, perhaps it wouldn't be best on the whole. Industry is a good teacher, and money cannot buy happiness, as I know to my sorrow."

The old gentleman still seemed to be talking to the frog, and as he spoke he took his hand out of his pocket with less in it than he had at first intended.

"What a very queer person!" thought Marjorie,

for she had not heard a word, and wondered what he was thinking about down there.

Jack walked out of the brook just then, and she ran to check him up; not an easy task for little hands, as he preferred to nibble the grass on the bank. But she did it cleverly, smoothed the ruffled mane, and, dropping another curtsy, stood aside to let the little carriage pass.

"Thank you, child — thank you. Here is something for your bank, and good luck to it."

As he spoke, the old man laid a bright gold dollar in her hand, patted the rosy cheek, and vanished in a cloud of dust, leaving Marjorie so astonished at the grandeur of the gift, that she stood looking at it as if it had been a fortune. It was to her; and visions of pink calico gowns, new grammars, and fresh hat-ribbons danced through her head in delightful confusion, as her eyes rested on the shining coin in her palm.

Then, with a solemn air, she invested her first money by popping it down the chimney of the scarlet mansion, and peeping in with one eye to see if it landed safely on the ground-floor. This done, she took a long breath, and looked over the railing, to be sure it was not all a dream. No; the wheelmarks were still there, the brown water was not yet clear, and, if a witness was needed, there sat the big frog again, looking so like the old gentleman, with his bottle-green coat, speckled trousers, and twinkling eyes, that Marjorie burst out laughing, and clapped her hands, saying aloud, —

"I'll play he was the Brownie, and this is the good-luck penny he gave me. Oh, what fun!" and away she skipped, rattling the dear new bank like a castanet.

When she had told granny all about it, she got knife and basket, and went out to dig dandelions; for the desire to increase her fortune was so strong, she could not rest a minute. Up and down she went, so busily peering and digging, that she never lifted up her eyes till something like a great white bird skimmed by so low she could not help seeing it. A pleasant laugh sounded behind her as she started up, and, looking round, she nearly sat down again in sheer surprise, for there close by was a slender little lady, comfortably established under a big umbrella.

"If there *were* any fairies, I'd be sure that was one," thought Marjorie, staring with all her might, for her mind was still full of the old story; and curious things do happen on birthdays, as every one knows.

It really did seem rather elfish to look up suddenly and see a lovely lady all in white, with shining hair and a wand in her hand, sitting under what looked very like a large yellow mushroom in the middle of a meadow, where, till now, nothing but cows and grasshoppers had been seen. Before Marjorie could decide the question, the pleasant laugh came again, and the stranger said, pointing to the white thing that was still fluttering over the grass like a little cloud, —

"Would you kindly catch my hat for me, before it blows quite away?"

Down went basket and knife, and away ran Marjorie, entirely satisfied now that there was no magic about the new-comer; for if she had been an elf, couldn't she have got her hat without any help from a mortal child? Presently, however, it did begin to seem as if that hat was bewitched, for it led the nimble-footed Marjorie such a chase that the cows stopped feeding to look on in placid wonder; the grasshoppers vainly tried to keep up, and every ox-eye daisy did its best to catch the runaway, but failed entirely, for the wind liked a game of romps, and had it that day. As she ran, Marjorie heard the lady singing, like the princess in the story of the Goose-Girl, —

> "Blow, breezes, blow!
> Let Curdkin's hat go!
> Blow, breezes, blow!
> Let him after it go!
> O'er hills, dales and rocks,
> Away be it whirled,
> Till the silvery locks
> Are all combed and curled."

This made her laugh so that she tumbled into a clover-bed, and lay there a minute to get her breath. Just then, as if the playful wind repented of its frolic, the long veil fastened to the hat caught in a blackberry-vine near by, and held the truant fast till Marjorie secured it.

"Now come and see what I am doing," said the lady, when she had thanked the child.

Marjorie drew near confidingly, and looked down at the wide-spread book before her. She gave a start, and laughed out with surprise and delight; for there was a lovely picture of her own little home, and her own little self on the door-step, all so delicate, and beautiful, and true, it seemed as if done by magic.

"Oh, how pretty! There is Rover, and Kitty and the robins, and me! How could you ever do it, ma'am?" said Marjorie, with a wondering glance at the long paint-brush, which had wrought what seemed a miracle to her childish eyes.

"I'll show you presently; but tell me, first, if it looks quite right and natural to you. Children sometimes spy out faults that no one else can see," answered the lady, evidently pleased with the artless praise her work received.

"It looks just like our house, only more beautiful. Perhaps that is because I know how shabby it really is. That moss looks lovely on the shingles, but the roof leaks. The porch is broken, only the roses hide the place; and my gown is all faded, though it once was as bright as you have made it. I wish the house and every thing would stay pretty forever as they will in the picture."

While Marjorie spoke, the lady had been adding more color to the sketch, and when she looked up, something warmer and brighter than sunshine shone in her face, as she said, so cheerily, it was like a bird's song to hear her, —

"It can't be summer always, dear, but we can make fair weather for ourselves if we try. The moss, the roses, and soft shadows show the little house and the little girl at their best, and that is what we all should do; for it is amazing how lovely common things become, if one only knows how to look at them."

"I wish *I* did," said Marjorie, half to herself, remembering how often she was discontented, and how hard it was to get on, sometimes.

"So do I," said the lady, in her happy voice. "Just believe that there is a sunny side to every thing, and try to find it, and you will be surprised to see how bright the world will seem, and how cheerful you will be able to keep your little self."

"I guess granny has found that out, for she never frets. I do, but I 'm going to stop it, because I 'm twelve to-day, and that is too old for such things," said Marjorie, recollecting the good resolutions she had made that morning when she woke.

"I am twice twelve, and not entirely cured yet; but I try, and don't mean to wear blue spectacles if I can help it," answered the lady, laughing so blithely that Marjorie was sure she would not have to try much longer. "Birthdays were made for presents, and I should like to give you one. Would it please you to have this little picture?" she added, lifting it out of the book.

"Truly my own? Oh, yes, indeed!" cried Marjorie, coloring with pleasure, for she had never owned so beautiful a thing before.

"Then you shall have it, dear. Hang it where you can see it often, and when you look, remember that it is the sunny side of home, and help to keep it so."

Marjorie had nothing but a kiss to offer by way of thanks, as the lovely sketch was put into her hand; but the giver seemed quite satisfied, for it was a very grateful little kiss. Then the child took up her basket and went away, not dancing and singing now, but slowly and silently; for this gift made her thoughtful as well as glad. As she climbed the wall, she looked back to nod good-by to the pretty lady; but the meadow was empty, and all she saw was the grass blowing in the wind.

"Now, deary, run out and play, for birthdays come but once a year, and we must make them as merry as we can," said granny, as she settled herself for her afternoon nap, when the Saturday cleaning was all done, and the little house as neat as wax.

So Marjorie put on a white apron in honor of the occasion, and, taking Kitty in her arms, went out to enjoy herself. Three swings on the gate seemed to be a good way of beginning the festivities; but she only got two, for when the gate creaked back the second time, it stayed shut, and Marjorie hung over the pickets, arrested by the sound of music.

"It's soldiers," she said, as the fife and drum drew nearer, and flags were seen waving over the barberry-bushes at the corner.

"No; it's a picnic," she added in a moment; for she saw hats with wreaths about them bobbing up and down, as a gayly-trimmed hay-cart full of children came rumbling down the lane.

"What a nice time they are going to have!" thought Marjorie, sadly contrasting that merry-making with the quiet party she was having all by herself.

Suddenly her face shone, and Kitty was waved over her head like a banner, as she flew out of the gate, crying, rapturously,—

"It's Billy! and I know he's come for me!"

It certainly *was* Billy, proudly driving the old horse, and beaming at his little friend from the bower of flags and chestnut-boughs, where he sat in state, with a crown of daisies on his sailor-hat and a spray of blooming sweetbrier in his hand. Waving his rustic sceptre, he led off the shout of "Happy birthday, Marjorie!" which was set up as the wagon stopped at the gate, and the green boughs suddenly blossomed with familiar faces, all smiling on the little damsel, who stood in the lane quite overpowered with delight.

"It's a s'prise party!" cried one small lad, tumbling out behind.

"We are going up the mountain to have fun!" added a chorus of voices, as a dozen hands beckoned wildly.

"We got it up on purpose for you, so tie your hat and come away," said a pretty girl, leaning down to kiss Marjorie, who had dropped Kitty, and stood ready for any splendid enterprise.

A word to granny, and away went the happy child, sitting up, beside Billy, under the flags that waved over a happier load than any royal chariot ever bore.

It would be vain to try and tell all the plays and pleasures of happy children on a Saturday afternoon, but we may briefly say that Marjorie found a mossy stone all ready for her throne, and Billy crowned her with a garland like his own. That a fine banquet was spread, and eaten with a relish many a Lord Mayor's feast has lacked. Then how the whole court danced and played together afterward! The lords climbed trees and turned somersaults, the ladies gathered flowers and told secrets under the sweetfern-bushes, the queen lost her shoe jumping over the waterfall, and the king paddled into the pool below and rescued it. A happy little kingdom, full of summer sunshine, innocent delights, and loyal hearts; for love ruled, and the only war that disturbed the peaceful land was waged by the mosquitoes as night came on.

Marjorie stood on her throne watching the sunset while her maids of honor packed up the remains of the banquet, and her knights prepared the chariot. All the sky was gold and purple, all the world bathed in a soft, red light, and the little girl was very happy as she looked down at the subjects who had served her so faithfully that day.

"Have you had a good time, Marjy?" asked King William; who stood below, with his royal nose on a level with her majesty's two dusty little shoes.

"Oh, Billy, it has been just splendid! But I don't see why you should all be so kind to me," answered Marjorie, with such a look of innocent wonder, that Billy laughed to see it.

"Because you are so sweet and good, we can't help loving you, — that's why," he said, as if this simple fact was reason enough.

"I'm going to be the best girl that ever was, and love everybody in the world," cried the child, stretching out her arms as if ready, in the fulness of her happy heart, to embrace all creation.

"Don't turn into an angel and fly away just yet, but come home, or granny will never lend you to us any more."

With that, Billy jumped her down, and away they ran, to ride gayly back through the twilight, singing like a flock of nightingales.

As she went to bed that night, Marjorie looked at the red bank, the pretty picture, and the daisy crown, saying to herself, —

"It has been a *very* nice birthday, and I am something like the girl in the story, after all, for the old man gave me a good-luck penny, the kind lady told me how to keep happy, and Billy came for me like the prince. The girl didn't go back to the poor house again, but I'm glad *I* did, for *my* granny isn't a cross one, and my little home is the dearest in the world."

Then she tied her night-cap, said her prayers,

and fell asleep; but the moon, looking in to kiss the blooming face upon the pillow, knew that three good spirits had come to help little Marjorie from that day forth, and their names were Industry, Cheerfulness, and Love.

IX.

PATTY'S PLACE.

I.

HOW SHE FOUND IT.

PATTY stood at one of the windows of the Asylum, looking thoughtfully down into the yard, where twenty girls were playing.

All had cropped heads, all wore brown gowns and blue aprons, and all were orphans like herself. Some were pretty and some plain, some rosy and gay, some pale and feeble, but all seemed happy and having a good time in spite of many drawbacks.

More than once one of them nodded and beckoned to Patty, but she shook her head decidedly, and still stood, listlessly watching them, and thinking to herself with a child's impatient spirit, —

"Oh, if some one would only come and take me away! I'm so tired of living here I don't think I *can* bear it much longer."

Poor Patty might well wish for a change; for she had been in the Asylum ever since she could remember; but though every one was kind to her, she was heartily tired of the place, and longed to find a home as many of the girls did.

The children were nursed and taught until old enough to help themselves, then were adopted by people or went out to service. Now and then some forlorn child was claimed by relatives who had discovered it, and once the relatives of a little girl proved to be rich and generous people, who came for Katy in a fine carriage, treated all the other girls in honor of the happy day, and from time to time let Katy visit them with hands full of gifts for her former playmates and friends.

This event had made a great stir in the Asylum, and the children were never tired of talking it over and telling it to new comers as a modern sort of fairy tale. For a time, each hoped to be claimed in the same way, and stories of what they would do when their turn came was one of the favorite amusements of the house.

By and by Katy ceased to come, and gradually new girls took the place of those that left, and her good fortune was forgotten by all but Patty. To her it always remained a splendid possibility, and she comforted her loneliness by visions of the day when her "folks" would come for her, and bear her away to a future of luxury and pleasure, rest and love.

But no one came, and year after year Patty worked and waited, saw others chosen and herself left to the many duties and few pleasures of her dull life. The reason why she was not taken was because of her pale face, her short figure, with one shoulder higher than the other, and her shy ways. She was not ill now, but looked so, and was a sober, quiet little woman at thirteen.

People who came for pets chose the pretty little ones; and those who wanted servants took the tall, strong, merry-faced girls, who spoke up brightly and promised to learn and do any thing required of them.

The good matron often recommended Patty as a neat, capable, gentle little person, but no one seemed to want her, and after every failure her heart grew heavier and her face sadder, for the thought of spending her life there was unbearable.

Nobody guessed what a world of hopes and thoughts and feelings was hidden under that blue pinafore, what dreams the solitary child enjoyed, or what a hungry, aspiring young soul lived in that crooked little body.

But God knew; and when the time came He remembered Patty and sent her the help best fitted for her needs. Sometimes, when we least expect it, a small cross proves a lovely crown, a seemingly unimportant event becomes a life-long experience, or a stranger changes into a friend.

It happened so now; for as Patty said aloud with a great sigh, "I don't think I *can* bear it any longer!" a hand touched her shoulder, and a voice said, gently, —

"Bear what, my child?"

The touch was so light and the voice so kind that Patty answered before she had time to feel shy.

"Living here, ma'am, and never being chosen out like the other girls are."

"Tell me all about it, dear. I'm waiting for a friend, and I'd like to hear your troubles," sitting down in the window-seat and drawing Patty beside her.

She was not young, nor pretty, nor finely dressed, only a gray-haired woman in plain black; but her face was so motherly, her eyes so cheerful, and her voice so soothing, that Patty felt at ease in a minute, and nestled up to her as she told her little woes in a few simple words.

"You don't know any thing about your parents?" asked the lady.

"No, ma'am; I was left here a baby without even a name pinned to me, and no one has come to find me. But I shouldn't wonder if they did yet, so I keep ready all the time and learn as hard as I can, so they won't be ashamed of me, for I guess my folks is respectable," and Patty lifted her head with an air of pride that made the lady ask, with a smile, —

"What makes you think so?"

"Well, I heard the matron tell a lady who chose Nelly Brian that she always thought *I* came of high folks because I was so different from the others, and my ways was nice, and my feet so small, —see if they ain't," — and, slipping them out of the rough shoes she wore, Patty held up two slender little feet with the arched insteps that tell of good birth.

Miss Murry laughed right out at the innocent vanity of the poor child, and said, heartily, "They *are* small, and so are your hands in spite of work, and your hair is fine, and your eyes are soft and clear, and you are a good child I'm sure, which is best of all."

Pleased and touched by the praise that is so pleasant to us all, yet half ashamed of herself, Patty blushed and smiled, put on her shoes, and said, with unusual animation, —

"I'm pretty good, I believe, and I know I'd be much better if I only could get out. I do so long to see trees and grass, and sit in the sun and hear birds. I'd work real hard and be happy if I could live in the country."

"What can you do?" asked Miss Murry, stroking the smooth head and looking down into the wistful eyes fixed upon her.

Modestly, but with a flutter of hope at her heart, Patty told over her domestic accomplishments, a good list for a thirteen-year-older, but Patty had been drilling so long she was unusually clever at all sorts of house-work as well as needle-work.

As she ended, she asked, timidly, —

"Did you come for a girl, ma'am?"

"My sister did; but she has found one she likes, and is going to take her on trial," was the answer that made the light fade out of Patty's eyes and the hope die in her heart.

"Who is it, please?"

"Lizzie Brown, a tall, nice-looking girl of fourteen."

"You won't like her I know, for Lizzie is a real

——;" there Patty stopped short, turned red, and looked down, as if ashamed to meet the keen, kind eyes fixed on her.

"A real what?"

"Please, ma'am, don't ask; it was mean of me to say that, and I mustn't go on. Lizzie can't help being good with you, and I am glad she 's got a chance to go away."

Miss Murry asked no more questions; but she liked the little glimpse of character, and tried to brighten Patty's face again by talking of something she liked.

"Suppose your 'folks,' as you say, never come for you, and you never find your fortune, as some girls do, can't you make friends and fortune for yourself?"

"How can I?" questioned Patty, wonderingly.

"By taking cheerfully whatever comes, by being helpful and affectionate to all, and wasting no time in dreaming about what may happen, but bravely making each day a comfort and a pleasure to yourself and others. Can you do that?"

"I can try, ma'am," answered Patty, meekly.

"I wish you would; and when I come again you can tell me how you get on. I think you will succeed; and when you do, you will have found a fine fortune, and be sure of friends. Now I must go; cheer up, deary, your turn must come some day."

With a kiss that won Patty's heart, Miss Murry went away, casting more than one look of pity at the little figure in the window-seat, sobbing, with a blue pinafore over its face.

This disappointment was doubly hard to Patty; because Lizzie was not a good girl, and deserved nothing, and Patty had taken a great fancy to the lady who spoke so kindly to her.

For a week after this she went about her work with a sad face, and all her day-dreams were of living with Miss Murry in the country.

Monday afternoon, as she stood sprinkling clothes, one of the girls burst in, saying, all in a breath, —

"Somebody's come for you, and you are to go right up to the parlor. It's Mrs. Murry, and she's brought Liz back, 'cause she told fibs, and was lazy, and Liz is as mad as hops, for it is a real nice place, with cows, and pigs, and children; and the work ain't hard and she wanted to stay. Do hurry, and don't stand staring at me that way."

"It can't be me — no one ever wants me — it's some mistake" — stammered Patty, so startled and excited, she did not know what to say or do.

"No, it isn't. Mrs. Murry won't have any one but *you*, and the matron says you are to come right up. Go along; I'll finish here. I'm *so* glad you have got a chance at last;" and with a good-natured hug, the girl pushed Patty out of the kitchen.

In a few minutes Patty came flying back, all in a twitter of delight, to report that she was going at once, and must say good-by all round. Every one was pleased, and when the flurry was over, the carriage drove away with the happiest little girl ever seen inside, for at last some one *did* want her, and Patty *had* found a place.

II.

HOW SHE FILLED IT.

For a year Patty lived with the Murrys, industrious, docile, and faithful, but not yet happy, because she had not found all she expected. They were kind to her, as far as plenty of food and not too much work went. They clothed her comfortably, let her go to church, and did not scold her very often. But no one showed that they loved her, no one praised her efforts, no one seemed to think that she had any hope or wish beyond her daily work, and no one saw in the shy, quiet little maid-servant, a lonely, tender-hearted girl longing for a crumb of the love so freely given to the children of the house.

The Murrys were busy people; the farm was large, and the master and his eldest son were hard at it all summer. Mrs. Murry was a brisk, smart housewife, who "flew round" herself, and expected others to do likewise. Pretty Ella, the daughter, was about Patty's age, and busy with her school, her little pleasures, and all the bright plans young girls love and live in. Two or three small lads rioted about the house, making much work, and doing very little.

One of these boys was lame, and this fact seemed to establish a sort of friendly understanding between him and Patty, for he was the only one who ever expressed any regard for her. She was very good to him, always ready to help him, always patient with his fretfulness, and always quick to understand his sensitive nature.

"She's only a servant, a charity girl who works for her board, and wears my old duds. She's good enough in her place, but of course she can't expect to be like one of us," Ella said to a young friend once, and Patty heard her.

"Only a servant"—that was the hard part, and it never occurred to any one to make it softer; so Patty plodded on, still hoping and dreaming about friends and fortune.

If it had not been for Miss Murry I fear the child would not have got on at all. But Aunt Jane never forgot her, though she lived twenty miles away, and seldom came to the farm. She wrote once a month, and always put in a little note to Patty, which she expected to have answered.

So Patty wrote a neat reply, very stiff and short at first; but after a time she quite poured out her heart to this one friend who sent her encouraging words, cheered her with praise now and then, and made her anxious to be all Miss Jane seemed to expect. No one took much notice of this correspondence, for Aunt Jane was odd, and Patty used to post her replies herself, being kindly provided with stamps by her friend.

This was Patty's anchor in her little sea of troubles, and she clung to it, hoping that some time, when she had earned such a beautiful reward, she would go and live with Miss Murry.

Christmas was coming, and great fun was expected; for the family were to pass the day before at Aunt Jane's, and bring her home for the dinner and dance next day. For a week beforehand, Mrs. Murry flew round with more than her accustomed speed, and Patty trotted from morning till night, lending a hand at all the least agreeable jobs. Ella did the light, pretty work, and spent much time over her new dress, and the gifts she was making for the boys.

Every thing was done at last, and Mrs. Murry declared that she should drop if she had another thing to do but go to Jane's and rest.

Patty had lived on the hope of going with them; but nothing was said about it, and they all trooped gayly away to the station, leaving her to take care of the house, and see that the cat did not touch one of the dozen pies stored away in the pantry.

Patty kept up bravely till they were gone; then she sat down like Cinderella, and cried, and cried until she couldn't cry any more, for it did seem as if she never was to have any fun, and no fairy godmother came to help her. The shower did her good, and she went about her work with a meek, patient face that would have touched a heart of stone.

All the morning she finished up the odd jobs left her to do, and in the afternoon, as the only approach to a holiday she dared venture, she sat at the parlor window and watched other people go to and fro, intent on merry-makings in which she had no part.

One pleasant little task she had, and that was arranging gifts for the small boys. Miss Jane had given her a bit of money now and then, and out of her meagre store the affectionate child had made presents for the lads; poor ones, but full of good-will and the desire to win some in return.

The evening was very long, for the family did not return as early as they expected to do, so Patty got out her treasure-box, and, sitting on the warm kitchen hearth, tried to amuse herself, while the wind howled outside and snow fell fast.

There we must leave her for a little while, quite unconscious of the happy surprise that was being prepared for her.

When Aunt Jane welcomed the family, her first word, as she emerged from a chaos of small boys' arms and legs, was "Why, where is Patty?"

"At home, of course; where should she be?" answered Mrs. Murry.

"Here with you. I said '*all come*' in my letter; didn't you understand it?"

"Goodness, Jane, you didn't mean bring her too, I hope."

"Yes, I did, and I'm so disappointed I'd go and get her if I had time."

Miss Jane knit her brows and looked vexed, as Ella laughed at the idea of a servant's going pleasuring with the family.

"It can't be helped now, so we'll say no more, and make it up to Patty to-morrow, if we can." And Aunt Jane smiled her own pleasant smile, and kissed the little lads all round, as if to sweeten her temper as soon as possible.

They had a capital time, and no one observed that Aunty now and then led the talk to Patty, asked a question about her, caught up every little hint dropped by the boys concerning her patience and kindness, and when Mrs. Murry said, as she sat resting, with a cushion at her back, a stool at her feet, and a cup of tea steaming deliciously under her nose, —

"Afraid to leave her there in charge? Oh, dear no! I've entire confidence in her, and she is equal to taking care of the house for a week if need be.

On the whole, Jane, I consider her a pretty promising girl. She isn't very quick, but she *is* faithful, steady, and honest as daylight."

"High praise from you, Maria; I hope she knows your good opinion of her."

"No, indeed; it don't do to pamper up a girl's pride by praising her. I say, 'Very well, Patty,' when I'm satisfied, and that's enough."

"Ah, but *you* wouldn't be satisfied if George only said, 'Very well, Maria,' when you had done your very best to please him in some way."

"That's a different thing," began Mrs. Murry, but Miss Jane shook her head, and Ella said, laughing, —

It's no use to try and convince Aunty on that point, she has taken a fancy to Pat, and won't see any fault in her. She's a good child enough; but I can't get any thing out of her, she is so odd and shy."

"I can; she's first rate, and takes care of me better than any one else," said Harry, the lame boy, with sudden warmth, for Patty had quite won his selfish little heart by many services.

"She'll make mother a nice helper as she grows up, and I consider it a good speculation. In four years she 'll be eighteen, and if she goes on doing so well, I shan't begrudge her wages," added Mr. Murry, who sat near by, with a small son on each knee.

"She 'd be quite pretty if she was straight, and plump, and jolly. But she is as sober as a deacon, and when her work is done, sits in a corner, watching us with her big eyes, as shy and mute as a mouse," said Ned, the big brother, lounging on the sofa.

"A dull, steady-going girl, just fitted for a servant, and no more," concluded Mrs. Murry, setting down her cup as if the subject was ended.

"You are quite mistaken, and I 'll prove it!" and up jumped Aunt Jane so energetically, that the boys laughed and the elders looked annoyed. Pulling out a portfolio, Aunt Jane untied a little bundle of letters, saying impressively, —

"Now listen, all of you, and see what has been going on under Patty's blue pinafore this year."

Then Miss Jane read the little letters one by one, and it was curious to see how the faces of the listeners woke up, grew attentive first, then touched, then self-reproachful, and finally how full of interest, and respect, and something very like affection for little Patty.

These letters were pathetic to read, as Aunty read them to listeners who could supply much that the writer generously left unsaid, and the involuntary comments of the hearers proved the truth of Patty's words.

"*Does* she envy me because I'm 'pretty and gay, and have a good time?' I never thought how hard it must be for her to see me have all the fun, and she all the work. She's a girl like me, though she does grub; and I might have done more for her than give her my old clothes, and let her help dress me when I go to a party," said Ella, hastily, as Aunt Jane laid down one letter in which poor Patty told of many "good times and she not in 'em."

"Sakes alive, if I'd known the child wanted me to kiss her now and then, as I do the rest, I'd have done it in a minute," said Mrs. Murry, with sudden softness in her sharp eyes, as Aunt Jane read this little bit, —

"I *am* grateful, but, oh! I'm so lonely, and it's so hard not to have any mother like the children. If Mrs. Murry would only kiss me good-night sometimes, it would do me more good than pretty clothes or nice victuals."

"I've been thinking I'd let her go to school a

spell, ever since I heard her showing Bob how to do his lessons. But mother didn't think she could spare her," broke in Mr. Murry, apologetically.

"If Ella would help a little, I guess I could. Anyway, we might try a while, since she is so eager to learn," added his wife, anxious not to seem unjust to sister Jane.

"Well, Joe laughed at her as well as me, when the boys hunched up their shoulders the way she does," cried conscience-stricken Bob, as he heard a sad little paragraph about her crooked figure, and learned that it came from lugging heavy babies at the Asylum.

"I cuffed 'em both for it, and *I* have always liked Patty," said Harry, in a moral tone, which moved Ned to say, —

"You'd be a selfish little rascal if you didn't, when she slaves so for you and gets no thanks for it. Now that I know how it tires her poor little back to carry wood and water, I shall do it of course. If she'd only told me, I'd have done it all the time."

And so it went on till the letters were done, and they knew Patty as she was, and each felt sorry that he or she had not found her out before. Aunt

Jane freed her mind upon the subject, and they talked it over till quite an enthusiastic state of feeling set in, and Patty was in danger of being killed with kindness.

It is astonishing how generous and kind people are when once waked up to a duty, a charity, or a wrong. Now, every one was eager to repair past neglect, and if Aunt Jane had not wisely restrained them, the young folks would have done something absurd.

They laid many nice little plans to surprise Patty, and each privately resolved not only to give her a Christmas gift, but, what was better, to turn over a new leaf for the new year.

All the way home they talked over their various projects, and the boys kept bouncing into Aunt Jane's seat, to ask advice about their funny ideas.

"It must have been rather lonesome for the poor little soul all day. I declare I wish we 'd taken her along," said Mrs. Murry, as they approached the house, through the softly-falling snow.

"She 's got a jolly good fire all ready for us, and that 's a mercy, for I 'm half frozen," said Harry, hopping up the step.

"Don't you think if I touch up my blue merino

it would fit Patty, and make a nice dress for to-morrow, with one of my white aprons?" whispered Ella, as she helped Aunt Jane out of the sleigh.

"Hope the child isn't sick or scared; it's two hours later than I expected to be at home," added Mr. Murry, stepping up to peep in at the kitchen window, for no one came to open the door, and no light but the blaze of the fire shone out.

"Come softly and look in; it's a pretty little sight, if it is in a kitchen," he whispered, beckoning to the rest.

Quietly creeping to the two low windows, they all looked in, and no one said a word, for the lonely little figure was both pretty and pathetic, when they remembered the letters lately read. Flat on the old rug lay Patty fast asleep; one arm pillowed her head, and in the other lay Puss in a cosy bunch, as if she had crept there to be sociable, since there was no one else to share Patty's long vigil. A row of slippers, large and small, stood warming on the hearth, two little nightgowns hung over a chair, the tea-pot stood in a warm nook, and through the open door they could see the lamp burning brightly in the sitting-room, the table ready, and all things in order.

"Faithful little creature! She's thought of every blessed thing, and I'll go right in and wake her up with a good kiss!" cried Mrs. Murry, making a dart at the door.

But Aunt Jane drew her back, begging her not to frighten the child by any sudden demonstrations. So they all went softly in, so softly that tired Patty did not wake, even though Puss pricked up her ears and opened her moony eyes with a lazy purr.

"Look here," whispered Bob, pointing to the poor little gifts half tumbling out of Patty's apron. She had been pinning names on them when she fell asleep, and so her secret was known too soon.

No one laughed at the presents, and Ella covered them up with a look of tender pity at the few humble treasures in Patty's box, remembering as she laid back what she had once called "rubbish," how full her own boxes were of the pretty things girls love, and how easy it would have been to add to Patty's store.

No one exactly knew how to wake up the sleeper, for she was something more than a servant in their eyes now. Aunt Jane settled the matter by stooping down and taking Patty in her arms. The big eyes opened at once and stared up at the face above them for a moment, then a smile so bright, so glad, shone all over the child's face that it was transfigured, as Patty clung to Aunt Jane, crying joyously, —

"Is it really you? I was so afraid you wouldn't come that I cried myself to sleep about it."

Never had any of them seen such love and happiness in Patty's face before, heard such a glad, tender sound in her voice, or guessed what an ardent soul lay in her quiet body.

She was herself again in a minute, and, jumping up, slipped away to see that every thing was ready, should any one want supper after the cold drive.

They all went to bed so soon that there was no time to let out the secret, and though Patty *was* surprised at the kind good-nights all said to her, she thought it was because Miss Jane brought a warmer atmosphere with her.

Patty's surprises began early next day; for the first thing she saw on opening her eyes was a pair of new stockings hanging at the foot of her bed, crammed full of gifts, and several parcels lying on the table.

Didn't she have a good time opening the delightful bundles? Didn't she laugh and cry at the droll things the boys gave, the comfortable and pretty things the elders sent? And wasn't she a happy child when she tried to say her prayers and couldn't find words beautiful enough to express her gratitude for so much kindness?

A new Patty went down stairs that morning, — a bright-faced girl with smiles on the mouth that used to be so sad and silent, confidence in the timid eyes, and the magic of the heartiest good-will to make her step light, her hand skilful, her labor a joy, and service no burden.

"They do care for me, after all, and I never will complain again," she thought, with a glad flutter at her heart, and sudden color in her cheeks, as every one welcomed her with a friendly "Merry Christmas, Patty!"

It *was* a merry Christmas, and when the bountiful dinner was spread and Patty stood ready to wait, you can imagine her feelings as Mr. Murry pointed to a seat near Miss Jane and said, in a fatherly tone that made his bluff voice sweet, —

"Sit down and enjoy it with us, my girl; nobody has more right to it, and we are all one family today."

Patty could not eat much, her heart was so full;

but it was a splendid feast to her, and when healths were drank she was overwhelmed by the honor Harry did her, for he bounced up and exclaimed, —

"Now we must drink 'Our Patty, long life and good luck to her!'"

That really *was* too much, and she fairly ran away to hide her blushes in the kitchen-roller, and work off her excitement washing dishes.

More surprises came that evening; when she went to put on her clean calico she found the pretty blue dress and white apron laid ready on her bed "with Ella's love."

"It 's like a fairy story, and keeps getting nicer and nicer since the godmother came," whispered Patty, as she shyly looked up at Aunt Jane, when passing ice-cream at the party several hours later.

"Christmas is the time for all sorts of pleasant miracles, for the good fairies fly about just then, and give good-luck pennies to the faithful workers who have earned them," answered Miss Jane, smiling back at her little handmaid, who looked so neat and blithe in her new suit and happy face.

Patty thought nothing farther in the way of bliss *could* happen to her that night, but it did when Ned, anxious to atone for his past neglect, pranced up to her, as a final contra-dance was forming, and said heartily, —

"Come, Patty, every one is to dance this, even Harry and the cat," and before she could collect her wits enough to say "No," she was leading off and flying down the middle with the young master in great style.

That was the crowning honor; for she was a girl with all a girl's innocent hopes, fears, desires and delights, and it *had* been rather hard to stand by while all the young neighbors were frolicking together.

When every one was gone, the tired children asleep, and the elders on their way up to bed, Mrs. Murry suddenly remembered she had not covered the kitchen fire. Aunt Jane said she would do it, and went down so softly that she did not disturb faithful Patty, who had gone to see that all was safe.

Aunt Jane stopped to watch the little figure standing on the hearth alone, looking into the embers with thoughtful eyes. If Patty could have seen her future there, she would have found a long life spent in glad service to those she loved and who loved her. Not a splendid future, but a useful, happy one; "only a servant," yet a good and faithful woman, blessed with the confidence, respect and affection of those who knew her genuine worth.

As a smile broke over Patty's face, Miss Jane said, with an arm round the little blue-gowned figure, —

"What are you dreaming and smiling about, deary? The friends that are to come for you some day, with a fine fortune in their pockets?"

"No, ma'am, I feel as if I'd found my folks, and I don't want any finer fortune than the love they've given me to-day. I'm trying to think how I can deserve it, and smiling because it's so beautiful and I'm so happy," answered Patty, looking up at her first friend with full eyes and a glad, grateful glance that made her lovely.

X.

THE AUTOBIOGRAPHY OF AN OMNIBUS.

I WAS born in Springfield, — excuse me if I don't mention how many years ago, for my memory is a little treacherous on some points, and it does not matter in the least. I was a gay young 'bus, with a long, red body, yellow wheels, and a picture of Washington on each side. Beautiful portraits, I assure you, with powdered hair, massive nose, and a cataract of shirt-frill inundating his buff vest. His coat and eyes were wonderfully blue, and he stared at the world in general with superb dignity, no matter how much mud might temporarily obscure his noble countenance.

Yes, I was an omnibus to be proud of; for my yellow wheels rumbled sonorously as they rolled; my cushions were soft, my springs elastic, and my varnish shone with a brilliancy which caused the human eye to wink as it regarded me.

Joe Quimby first mounted my lofty perch, four

fine gray horses drew me from obscurity, and Bill Buffum hung gayly on behind as conductor; for in my early days there were no straps to jerk, and passengers did not plunge in and out in the undignified way they do now.

How well I remember my first trip, one bright spring day! I was to run between Roxbury and Boston, and we set out in great style, and an admiring crowd to see us off. That was the beginning of a long and varied career, — a useful one too, I hope; for never did an omnibus desire to do its duty more sincerely than I did. My heart yearned over every one whom I saw plodding along in the dust; my door opened hospitably to rich and poor, and no hand beckoned to me in vain. Can every one say as much?

For years I trundled to and fro punctually at my appointed hours, and many curious things I saw — many interesting people I carried. Of course, I had my favorites, and though I did my duty faithfully to all, there were certain persons whom I loved to carry, whom I watched for and received into my capacious bosom with delight.

Several portly old gentlemen rode down to their business every day for years, and I felt myself honored by such eminently respectable passengers. Nice, motherly women, with little baskets, daily went to market; for in earlier days housewives attended to these matters and were notable managers. Gay young fellows would come swarming up beside Joe, and crack jokes all the way into town, amusing me immensely.

But my especial pets were the young girls,—for we had girls then,—blithe, bonny creatures, with health on their cheeks, modesty in their bright eyes, and the indescribable charm of real maidenliness about them. So simply dressed, so quiet in manner, so unconscious of display, and so full of innocent gayety, that the crustiest passenger could not help softening as they came in. Bless their dear hearts! what would they say if they could see the little fashion-plates school-girls are now? The seven-story hats with jet daggers, steel arrows, and gilt horse-shoes on the sides, peacocks' tails in front, and quantities of impossible flowers tumbling off behind. The jewelry, the frills and bows, the frizzled hair and high-heeled boots, and, worst of all, the pale faces, tired eyes, and ungirlish manners.

Well, well, I must not scold the poor dears, for they are only what the times make them,—fast and loud, frivolous and feeble. All are not spoilt, thank heaven; for now and then, a fresh, modest face goes by, and then one sees how lovely girlhood may be.

I saw many little romances, and some small tragedies, in my early days, and learned to take such interest in human beings, that I have never been able to become a mere machine.

When one of my worthy old gentlemen dropped away, and I saw him no more, I mourned for him like a friend. When one of my housewifely women came in with a black bonnet on, and no little lad or lass clinging to her hand, I creaked my sympathy for her loss, and tried not to jolt the poor mother whose heart was so heavy. When one of my pretty girls entered, blushing and smiling, with a lover close behind, I was as pleased and proud as if she had been my own, and every black button that studded my red cushion twinkled with satisfaction.

I had many warm friends among the boys who were allowed to "hang on behind," for I never gave a dangerous lurch when they were there, and never pinched their fingers in the door. No, I gave a jolly rumble when the steps were full; and I kept the father of his country beaming so benignly at them that they learned to love his old face, to watch for it, and to cheer it as we went by.

I was a patriotic 'bus; so you may imagine my feelings when, after years of faithful service on that route, I was taken off and sent to the paint-shop, where a simpering damsel, with lilies in her hair, replaced G. Washington's honored countenance. I was re-christened "The Naiad Queen," which disgusted me extremely, and kept to carry picnic parties to a certain lake.

Earlier in my life I should have enjoyed the fun; but I was now a middle-aged 'bus, and felt as if I wanted more serious work to do. However, I resigned myself and soon found that the change did me good; for in the city I was in danger of getting grimy with mud, battered with banging over stones, and used up with the late hours, noise and excitement of town life.

Now I found great refreshment in carrying loads of gay young people into the country for a day of sunshine, green grass, and healthful pleasure. What jolly parties they were, to be sure! Such laughing and singing, feasting and frolicking; such baskets of flowers and fresh boughs as they carried home;

and, better still, such blooming cheeks, happy eyes, and hearts bubbling over with the innocent gayety of youth! They soon seemed as fond of me as I was of them, for they welcomed me with shouts when I came, played games and had banquets inside of me when sun or rain made shelter pleasant, trimmed me up with wreaths as we went home in triumph, and gave three rousing cheers for the old 'bus when we parted. That was a happy time, and it furnished many a pleasant memory for duller days.

After several seasons of picnicking, I was taken to an asylum for the deaf, dumb, and blind, and daily took a dozen or so out for an airing. You can easily imagine this was a great contrast to my last place; for now, instead of rollicking parties of boys and girls, I took a sad load of affliction; and it grieved me much to know that while some of the poor little creatures could see nothing of the beauty round them, the others could hear none of the sweet summer sounds, and had no power to express their happiness in blithe laughter or the gay chatter one so loves to hear.

But it did me good; for, seeing them so patient with their great troubles, I was ashamed to grumble about my small ones. I was now getting to be an elderly 'bus, with twinges of rheumatism in my axletrees, many cracks like wrinkles on my once smooth paint, and an asthmatic creak to the hinges of the door that used to swing so smartly to and fro. Yes, I was evidently getting old, for I began to think over my past, to recall the many passengers I had carried, the crusty or jolly coachmen I had known, the various horses who had tugged me over stony streets or dusty roads, and the narrow escapes I had had in the course of my career.

Presently I found plenty of time for such reminiscences, for I was put away in an old stable and left there undisturbed a long, long time. At first, I enjoyed the rest and quiet; but I was of a social turn, and soon longed for the stirring life I had left. I had no friends but a few gray hens, who roosted on my pole, laid eggs in the musty straw on my floor, and came hopping gravely down my steps with important "cut, cut, ka da cuts!" when their duty was done. I respected these worthy fowls, and had many a gossip with them; but their views were very limited, and I soon tired of their domestic chat.

Chanticleer was coachman now, as in the days of Partlet and the nuts; but he never drove out, only flew up to my roof when he crowed, and sat there, in his black and yellow suit, like a diligence-driver sounding his horn. Interesting broods of chickens were hatched inside, and took their first look at life from my dingy windows. I felt a grand-fatherly fondness for the downy things, and liked to have them chirping and scratching about me, taking small flights from my steps, and giving funny little crows in imitation of their splendid papa.

Sundry cats called often, for rats and mice haunted the stable, and these gray-coated huntsmen had many an exciting chase among my moth-eaten cushions, over the lofts, and round the grain-bags.

"Here I shall end my days," I thought, and resigned myself to obscurity. But I was mistaken; for just as I was falling out of one long doze into another, a terrible commotion among the cats, hens, and mice woke me up, and I found myself trundling off to the paint-shop again.

I emerged from that fragrant place in a new scarlet coat, trimmed with black and ornamented with a startling picture of a salmon-colored Mazeppa, airily dressed in chains and a blue sheet, hanging by one foot to the back of a coal-black steed with red nostrils and a tempestuous tail, who was wildly careering over a range of pea-green mountains on four impossible legs. It was much admired; but I preferred George Washington, like the loyal 'bus that I am.

I found I was to live in the suburbs and carry people to and from the station of a new railway, which, with the town, seemed to have sprung up like mushrooms. Well, I bumped passengers about the half-finished streets; but I did not like it, for every thing had changed much during my retirement. Everybody seemed in a tearing hurry now, — the men to be rich, the women to be fine; the boys and girls couldn't wait to grow up, but flirted before they were in their teens; and the very babies scrambled out of their cradles as if each was bent on toddling farther and faster than its neighbor. My old head quite spun round at the whirl every thing was in, and my old wheels knew no rest, for the new coachman drove like Jehu.

It is my private opinion that I should soon have fallen to pieces if a grand smash had not settled the matter for me. A gay young fellow undertook to drive, one dark night, and upset his load in a ditch, fortunately breaking no bones but mine. So I was sent to a carriage factory for repairs; but

ently, my injuries were past cure, for I was left on a bit of waste land behind the factory, to go to ruin at leisure.

"This is the end of all things," I said, with a sigh, as year after year went by and I stood there alone, covered with wintry snow or blistered by summer sunshine. But how mistaken I was! for just when all seemed most sad and solitary, the happiest experience of my life came to me, and all the world was brightened for me by the coming of my dearest friends.

One chilly spring night, when rain was falling, and the wind sighed dismally over the flats, I was waked from a nap by voices and the rustling of straw inside my still strong body.

"Some tramp," I thought, with a yawn, for I had often taken lodgers for a night, rent free. But the sounds I now heard were the voices of children, and I listened with interest to the little creatures chirping and nestling in there like the chickens I told you of.

"It's as nice as a house, Hans, and so warm I'll soon be dry," said one of the homeless birds who had taken shelter in my bosom.

"It's nicer than a house, Gretchen, because we

can push it about if we like. I wish we could stay here always; I'm so tired of the streets," sighed another young voice.

"And I'm so hungry; I do wish mother would come," cried a very tired baby voice, with a sob.

"Hush, go to sleep, my Lina! I'll wake you if mother brings us bread, and if not you will feel no disappointment, dear."

Then the elder sister seemed to wrap the little one close, and out of my bosom came a soft lullaby, as one child gave the other all she had, — love and care.

"In the shed yonder I saw a piece of carpet; I shall go and bring it to cover us, then you will not shiver so, dear Gretchen," said the boy; and out into the rainy darkness he went, whistling to keep his spirits up and hide his hunger.

Soon he came hurrying back with the rude coverlet, and another voice was heard, saying, in the tone that only mothers use, —

"Here is supper, dear children. Eat all; I have no wish for any more. People were very good to me, and there is enough for every one."

Then, with cries of joy, the hungry birds were fed, the motherly wings folded over them, and all seemed to sleep in the poor nest they had found.

All night the rain pattered on my old roof, but not a drop went through; all night the chilly wind crept round my windows, and breathed in at every broken pane, but the old carpet kept the sleepers warm, and weariness was a sure lullaby. How pleased and proud I felt that I could still be useful, and how eagerly I waited for day to see yet more of my new tenants! I knew they would go soon and leave me to my loneliness, so I longed to see and hear all I could.

The first words the mother said, as she sat upon the step in the warm April sun, pleased me immensely, for they were of me.

"Yes, Hans, it will be well to stay here a day at least, if we may, for Lina is worn out and poor Gretchen so tired she can go no more. You shall guard them while they sleep, and I will go again for food, and may get work. It is better out here in the sun than in some poor place in the city, and I like it well, this friendly old carriage that sheltered us when most we needed it."

So the poor woman trudged away, like a true mother-bird, to find food for the ever-hungry brood, and Hans, a stout lad of twelve, set about doing his part manfully.

When he heard the workmen stirring in the great factory, he took courage, and, going in, told his sad talè of the little tired sisters sleeping in the old omnibus, the mother seeking work, the father lately dead, and he (the young lad) left to guard and help the family. He asked for nothing but leave to use the bit of carpet, and for any little job whereby he might earn a penny.

The good fellows had fatherly hearts under their rough jackets, and lent a helping hand with the readiness the poor so often show in lightening one another's burdens. Each did what he could; and when the mother came back, she found the children fed and warmed, cheered by kind words and the promise of help.

Ah! it was a happy day for me when the Schmidts came wandering by and found my door ajar! A yet happier one for them, since the workmen and their master befriended the poor souls so well that in a week the houseless family had a home, and work whereby to earn their bread.

They had taken a fancy to me, and I was their home; for they were a hardy set and loved the sun and air. Clever Hans and his mother made me as neat and cosy as possible, stowing away their few possessions as if on shipboard. The shed was given to mother Schmidt for a wash-house, and a gypsy fire built on the ground, with an old kettle slung over it, in which to boil the clothes she washed for such of the men as had no wives. Hans and Gretchen soon found work selling chips and shavings from the factory, and bringing home the broken food they begged by the way. Baby Lina was a universal pet, and many a sixpence found its way into her little hand from the pockets of the kindly men, who took it out in kisses, or the pretty songs she sang them.

All that summer my family prospered, and I was a happy old 'bus. A proud one, too; for the dear people loved me well, and, in return for the shelter I gave them, they beautified me by all the humble means in their power. Some one gave Gretchen a few scarlet beans, and these she planted among the dandelions and green grass that had grown about my wheels. The gay runners climbed fast, and when they reached the roof, Hans made a trellis of old barrel hoops, over which they spread their broad leaves and bright flowers till Lina had a green little bower up aloft, where she sat, as happy as a queen, with the poor toys which her baby fancy changed to playthings of the loveliest sort.

Mother Schmidt washed and ironed busily all day in her shed, cooked the soup over her gypsy fire, and when the daily work was done sat in the shadow of the old omnibus with her children round her, a grateful and contented woman. If any one asked her what she would do when our bitter winter came, the smile on her placid face grew graver, but did not vanish, as she laid her worn hands together and answered, with simple faith, —

"The good Gott who gave us this home and raised up these friends will not forget us, for He has such as we in His especial charge."

She was right; for the master of the great factory was a kind man, and something in the honest, hard-working family interested him so much that he could not let them suffer, but took such friendly thought for them that he wrought one of the pleasant miracles which keep a rich man's memory green in grateful hearts, though the world may never know of it.

When autumn came and the pretty bower began to fade, the old omnibus to be cold at night, and the shed too gusty even for the hardy German laundress, a great surprise was planned and gayly carried out. On the master's birthday the men had a holiday, and bade the Schmidts be ready to take part in the festival, for all the factory people were to have a dinner in one of the long rooms.

A jovial time they had; and when the last bone had been polished off, the last health drunk, and three rousing cheers for the master given with a will, the great joke took place. First the Schmidts were told to go and see what had been left for them in the 'bus, and off they ran, little dreaming what was to come. *I* knew all about it, and was in a great twitter, for I bore a grand part in it.

The dear unsuspecting family piled in, and were so busy having raptures over certain bundles of warm clothes found there that they did not mind what went on without. A dozen of the stoutest men quietly harnessed themselves to the rope fastened to my pole, and at a signal trotted away with me at a great pace, while the rest, with their wives and children, came laughing and shouting after.

Imagine the amazement of the good Schmidts at this sudden start, their emotions during that triumphal progress, and their unspeakable surprise and joy when their carriage stopped at the door of a tidy little house in a lane not far away, and they were handed out to find the master waiting to welcome them home.

Dear heart, how beautiful it all was! I cannot describe it, but I would not have missed it for the world, because it was one of the scenes that do everybody so much good and leave such a pleasant memory behind.

That was my last trip, for the joyful agitation of that day was too much for me, and no sooner was I safely landed in the field behind the little house than one of my old wheels fell all to pieces, and I should have tumbled over, like a decrepit old creature, if the men had not propped me up. But I did not care; my travelling days were past, and I was quite content to stand there under the apple-trees, watching my family safe and busy in their new home.

I was not forgotten, I assure you; for Germans have much sentiment, and they still loved the old omnibus that sheltered them when most forlorn. Even when Hans was a worker in the factory he found time to mend me up and keep me tidy; pretty Gretchen, in spite of much help given to the hard-working mother, never forgot to plant some common flower to beautify and cheer her old friend;

and little Lina, bless her heart! made me her baby-house. She played there day after day, a tiny matron, with her dolls, her kitten and her bits of furniture, as happy a child as ever sang "Bye-low" to a dirty-faced rag-darling. She is my greatest comfort and delight; and the proudest moment of my life was when Hans painted her little name on my door and gave me to her for her own.

Here my story ends; for nothing now remains to me but to crumble slowly to ruin and go where the good 'busses go; very slowly, I am sure, for my little mistress takes great care of me, and I shall never suffer from rough usage any more. I am quite happy and contented as I stand here under the trees that scatter their white petals on my rusty roof each spring; and well I may be, for after my busy life I am at rest; the sun shines kindly on me, the grass grows greenly round me, good friends cherish me in my old age, and a little child nestles in my heart, keeping it tender to the last.

XI.

RED TULIPS.

"PLEASE, ma'am, will you give me one of them red tulips?"

The eager voice woke Helen from her reverie, and, looking up, she saw a little colored girl holding on to the iron railing with one hand, while the other pointed to a bed of splendid red and yellow tulips waving in the sunshine.

"I can't give you one, child, for they don't belong to me," answered Helen, arrested by the wistful face, over which her words brought a shadow of disappointment.

"I thought maybe you lived in this house, or knew the folks, and I *do* want one of them flowers dreadful bad," said the girl, regarding the gay tulips with a look of intense desire.

"I wish I *could* give you one, but it would be stealing, you know. Perhaps if you go and ask, the owner may let you have one, there are so many."

And having offered all the consolation in her

power, Helen went on, busy with a certain disappointment of her own, which just then weighed very heavily on her girlish heart.

Half an hour later, as she came down the street on the opposite side, she saw the same girl sitting on a door-step, still gazing at the tulips with hopeless admiration.

The child looked up as she approached, and recognizing the pretty young lady who had spoken kindly to her, smiled and nodded so confidingly, that Helen could not resist stopping to say,—

"Did you ask over there?"

"Yes, ma'am, but the girl said, 'No,' and told me to clear out; so I come over here to set and look at the pretties, since I can't have none," she answered, with a patient sigh.

"You *shall* have some!" cried Helen, remembering how easily she could gratify the innocent longing of the poor child, and feeling a curious sympathy with all disappointed people. "Come with me, dear; there is a flower shop round the corner, and you shall have a posy of some sort."

Such wonder, gratitude and delight shone in Betty's face, that Helen felt rejoiced for her small kindness. As they walked, she questioned her about herself, and quite won her heart by the friendly interest expressed in Betty's mother, Betty's kitten, and Betty's affairs generally.

When they came to the flower shop little Bet felt as if she had got into a fairy tale; and when Helen gave her a pot with a blue hyacinth and a rosy tulip blooming prettily together, she felt as if a lovely fairy had granted all her wishes in the good old way.

"It's just splendid! and I don't know how to thank you, miss. But mother takes in washing, and she'll love to do yours, and plait the ruffles elegant — 'cause you done this for me!" cried Betty, embracing the flower-pot with one hand, and squeezing Miss Helen's with the other.

Helen promised to come and see her new friend, and when they parted, kept turning round to watch the little figure trotting up the hill, often pausing to turn, and show her a beaming black face, all smiles and delight, as Betty threw her kisses and hugged the dear red tulip like a treasure of great price.

When she vanished, Helen said to herself, with a smile and a sigh, —

"There, I feel better for that little job; and it

is a comfort to know that some one has got what she wants, though it is not I."

Some weeks later, when Helen was preparing to go into the country for the summer, and wanted certain delicate muslins done up, she remembered what Betty had said about her mother, and had a fancy to see how the child and her flowers prospered.

She found them in a small, poor room, hot and close, and full of wash-tubs and flat-irons. The mother was busy at her work, and Betty sat by the one window, listlessly picking out ruffles.

When she saw the face at the door, she jumped up and clapped her hands, crying, delightedly, "O mammy, it 's my lady; my dear, pretty lady truly come at last!"

Such a welcome made friends of the three at once, and Mrs. Simms gladly undertook the work Helen offered.

"And how are the posies?" asked the young lady, as she rose to go.

"Only leaves now, miss; but I take real good care of 'em, and mammy says they will blow again next spring," answered Betty, showing her poor little garden, which consisted of the hyacinth, tulip, and one stout dandelion, blooming bravely in an old teapot.

"That will be a long time to wait, won't it?"

"Yes'm; but I go and take peeks at them flowers in the shop, and once the man gave me a pink that hadn't no stem. Maybe he will again, and so I'll get along," said Betty, softly touching her cheerful dandelion as if it were a friend.

"I wish you would come and see my garden, little Betty. You should pick as many flowers as you liked, and play there all day long. I suppose your mother couldn't spare you for a visit, could she?"

Betty's face shone at the blissful thought, then the smile faded, and she shook her head, saying, steadily, "No, miss, I guess she couldn't, for she gets so tired, I like to help her by carrying home the clothes. Some day, maybe, I can come."

Something in the patient little face touched Helen, and made her feel as if she had been too busy thinking of her own burden to help others bear theirs. She longed to do something, but did not know how till Mrs. Simms showed her the way, by saying, as she stroked the frizzly little head that leaned against her, —

"Betty thinks a heap of flowers, and 'pears to git lots of comfort out of 'em. She's a good child, and some day we are going to see the country, soon as ever we can afford it."

"Meantime the country must come to you," said Helen, with a happy thought shining in her face. "If you are willing, I will make a nice little plan with Betty, so she can have a posy all the time. I shall come in town twice a week to take my German lessons, and if Betty will be at the corner of the Park, by the deer, every Wednesday and Saturday morning at ten o'clock, I'll have a nice nosegay for her."

If she had proposed to present the child with all the sweeties in Copeland's delightful shop, it would not have given greater joy. Betty could only dance a jig of rapture among the wash-tubs, and Mrs. Simms thank Helen with tears in her eyes.

"Ain't she just like a good fairy, mammy?" said Betty, settling down in an empty clothes-basket to brood over the joyful prospects.

"No, honey, she's an angel," answered mammy, folding her tired hands for a moment's rest, when her guest had gone.

Helen heard both question and answer, and sighed to herself, "I wish somebody else thought so."

When the first Wednesday came, Betty was at the trysting-place half an hour too soon, and had time to tell the mild-eyed deer all about it, before Miss Helen came.

That meeting was a pretty sight, though only a fawn and an old apple-woman saw it. Helen was half-hidden behind a great nosegay of June roses, lilies of the valley, sweet jonquils and narcissus, sprays of tender green, and white lilac plumes. Betty gave one cry of rapture, as she clutched it in both hands, trembling with delight, for never had she dreamed of owning such a treasure as this.

"All for me! all for me!" she said, as if it was hard to believe. "Oh, what *will* mammy say?"

"Run home and see. Never mind thanks. Get your posy into water as soon as you can, and come again Saturday," said Helen, as she went on, with a nod and a smile, while Betty raced home to fill every cup and plate they owned, and make a garden of the poor little room, where mammy worked all day.

All through the summer, rain or shine, these two friends kept tryst, and though Helen seemed no nearer getting her wish, this little flower-mission of hers helped her to wait.

Strangers watched the pretty girl with her nosegays, and felt refreshed by the winsome sight. Friends joked her about her black Flora, and would-be lovers pleaded in vain for one bud from her bouquets.

She found real happiness in this small duty, and did it faithfully for its own sake, little dreaming that some one was tracking her by the flowers she left behind her in the byways of her life.

For, seeing how much these fragrant messengers were to Betty and her mother, Helen fell into the way of taking flowers to others also, and never went to town without a handful to leave here and there, by some sick-bed, in a child's hand, on a needle-woman's table, or dropped in the gutter, for dear, dirty babies to find and crow over.

And, all unconsciously, these glimpses of poverty, pain, neglect, and loneliness, taught her lessons she had never learned before,—a sweeter language than German, a nobler music than any Herr Pedalstrum could give her, and a more winning charm than either youth or beauty could confer,—for the gay girl was discovering that life was not all a summer day, and she was something better than a butterfly.

When autumn came, and she returned to her city home, her young friends discovered that Helen's quiet season had improved her wonderfully, for behind the belle, they found a tender-hearted woman.

She took up her old life where she laid it down, apparently; but to those who knew her best, there was a difference now, for, in many unsuspected ways, pretty Helen was unconsciously fitting herself for the happiness that was coming to her very soon.

Betty helped to bring it, though she never guessed that her measles were a blessing to her dear lady. When Dr. Strong, finding a hot-house bouquet beside her bed, very naturally asked where it came from, Betty told all about Miss Helen, from the time of the red tulips to the fine tea-roses in her hand.

"She has lots of bunches like these sent to her, and she gives 'em to us poor folks. This one was for her to take to a splendid ball, but she kept it all fresh, and came herself to fetch it to me. Ain't she kind?"

"Very, to you; but rather cruel to the gentlemen

who hope to see her wear their gifts, for one evening at least," answered the doctor, examining the bouquet, with an odd smile.

"Oh, she does keep some, when they are from folks she likes. I was there one day when some violets come in with a book, and she wouldn't give me one. But I didn't care a mite, for I had two great posies, all red geranium and pinks, instead."

"She likes violets, then?" and the doctor gently patted Betty's head, as if he had grown suddenly fond of her.

"I guess she does, for when I went the next week, that very bunch was in the vase on her table, all dead and yeller, and she wouldn't let me fling it away, when I wanted to put in a rose from the bush she gave me."

"You are a grateful little girl, my dear, and a very observing child. Now keep warm and quiet, and we 'll have you trotting off to Miss Helen's in a week or so."

The doctor stole a sprig of rose geranium out of Betty's last bouquet, and went away, looking as if he had found something even sweeter than that in the dingy room where his patient lay.

Next day Miss Helen had fresh violets in the vase

on her table, and fresh roses blooming on her cheeks. Dr. Strong advised her not to visit Betty, as there was fever in the neighborhood, but kindly called every day or two, to let Helen know how her little friend was getting on.

After one of these calls, the doctor went away, saying to himself, with an air of tender pride and satisfaction, —

"I was mistaken, and judged too hastily last year. Helen is not what I thought her, a frivolous, fashionable beauty, but a sweet, sensible girl, who is tired of that empty life, and quietly tries to make it beautiful and useful in the best and truest way. I hope I read the blue eyes right; and I think I may venture to say now what I dared not say last year."

After that same visit, Helen sat thinking to herself, with a face full of happiness and humility, — "He finds me improved, so I have not waited in vain, and I believe that I shall not be disappointed after all."

It is evident that the doctor did venture, and that Helen was not disappointed; for, on the first day of June, Betty and her mother, all in their best, went to a certain church, and were shown to the best seat in the gallery, where several other humble friends were gathered to see their dear Miss Helen married.

Betty was in high feather, with a pink dress, blue sack, yellow ribbons in her hat, and lighted up the seat like an animated rainbow. Full of delight and importance, was Miss Betty, for she had been in the midst of the festive preparations, and told glowing tales to her interested listeners, while they waited for the bride.

When the music sounded, Betty held her breath, and rolled up her eyes in a pious rapture. When a general stir announced the grand arrival, she leaned so far over the gallery, that she would have gone head first if her mother had not caught her striped legs, and when the misty, white figure passed up the aisle, Betty audibly remarked, —

"If she had wings she 'd look like an out-and-out angel, wouldn't she, mammy?"

She sat like a little ebony statue all through the service; but she had something on her mind, and the moment the bridal couple turned to go out, Betty was off, scrambling down stairs, dodging under people's arms, hopping over ladies' skirts, and steadily making her way to the carriage waiting for the happy pair.

The door had just closed, and Dr. Strong was about to draw down the curtain, when a little black face, with a yellow hat surrounding it like a glory, appeared at the window, an arm was thrust in offering a bunch of flowers, and a breathless voice cried, resolutely, —

"Oh, please, do let me give 'em to my lady! They bloomed a-purpose for her, and she *must* have 'em."

Those outside saw a sweet face bend to kiss the little black one, but they did not see what happened afterward, for Helen, remembering a year ago, said smiling, —

"Patient waiters are no losers. The poor child has red tulips all her own at last!"

"And I have mine," answered the happy doctor, gently kissing his young wife, as the carriage rolled away, leaving Betty to retire in triumph.

XII.

A HAPPY BIRTHDAY.

A CERTAIN fine old lady was seventy-three on the 8th of October. The day was always celebrated with splendor by her children and grandchildren; but on this occasion they felt that something unusually interesting and festive should be done, because grandma had lately been so very ill that no one thought she would ever see another birthday. It pleased God to spare her, however, and here she was, almost as well and gay as ever.

Some families do not celebrate these days, and so miss a great deal of pleasure, I think. But the people of whom I write always made a great deal of such occasions, and often got up very funny amusements, as you will see.

As grandma was not very strong, some quiet fun must be devised this time, and the surprises sprinkled along through the day, lest they should be too much for her if they all burst upon her at once.

The morning was fine and clear, and the first thing that happened was the appearance of two little ghosts, "all in white," who came prancing into the old lady's room, while she lay placidly watching the sun rise, and thinking of the many years she had seen.

"A happy birthday, gramma!" cried the little ghosts, scrambling up to kiss the smiling old face in the ruffled night-cap.

There was a great laughing, and cuddling, and nestling among the pillows, before the small arms and legs subsided, and two round, rosy faces appeared, listening attentively to the stories grandma told them till it was time to dress.

Now you must know that there were only two grandchildren in this family, but they were equal to half a dozen, being lively, droll little chaps, full of all manner of pranks, and considered by their relatives the *most* remarkable boys alive.

These two fellows were quite bursting with the great secrets of the day, and had to rush out as soon as breakfast was done, in order to keep from "letting the cat out of the bag."

A fine dinner was cooked, and grandma's favorite niece came to eat it with her, bringing a bag full of goodies, and a heart full of love and kind wishes, to the old lady.

All the afternoon, friends and presents kept coming, and Madam, in her best gown and most imposing cap, sat in state to receive them. A poet came with some lovely flowers; the doctor brought a fine picture; one neighbor sent her a basket of grapes; another took her a drive; and some poor children, whom grandma had clothed and helped, sent her some nuts they had picked all themselves, while their grateful mother brought a bottle of cream and a dozen eggs.

It was very pleasant, and the bright autumn day was a little harvest time for the old lady, who had sowed love and charity broadcast with no thought of any reward.

The tea-table was ornamented with a splendid cake, white as snow outside, but rich and plummy inside, with a gay posy stuck atop of the little Mont Blanc. Mrs. Trot, the housekeeper, made and presented it, and it was so pretty all voted not to cut it till evening, for the table was full of other good things.

Grandma's tea was extra strong, and tasted unusually nice with Mrs. Hosy's rich cream in it. She felt that she needed this refreshment to prepare her for the grand surprise to come; for the family gifts were not yet given.

The boys vanished directly after tea, and shouts of laughter were heard from Aunt Tribulation's room. What larks as they had up there no one knew; but every one was sure they were preparing some fun in honor of the occasion.

Grandma was not allowed to go into the study, and much tacking and rummaging went on for a time. Then all the lamps were collected there, leaving grandma and grandpa to sit in the parlor, talking tenderly together by the soft glimmer of fire-light, as they used to do forty years ago.

Presently something scarlet and gold, feathery and strange, flitted by the door and vanished in the study. Queer little yells and the sound of dancing feet were heard. Then there was a hunt for the cat; next, Mrs. Trot was called from the kitchen, and all but the boys came to escort grandma to the scene of glory.

Leaning on grandpa's arm, she marched first; then came Mrs. Coobiddy, the mother of the boys, bearing Aunt Carmine's picture; for this auntie was over the water and could not come, so, at grandma's desire, her portrait was borne in the procession.

Aunt Trib followed, escorted by Thomas Pib, the great cat, with his best red bow on. Mrs. Trot and Belinda, the little maid, brought up the rear. A music-box in the hall played the "Grand March" from "Norma;" and, with great dignity, all filed into the study to behold an imposing spectacle.

A fire burned brightly on the hearth, making the old-fashioned andirons shine like gold. All the lamps illuminated the room, which was trimmed with scarlet and yellow leaves. An arch of red woodbine, evergreen and ferns from the White Mountains was made over the recess which held the journals, letters and books of the family; for their name was Penn, and they all wrote so much that blots were found everywhere about the house, and a flock of geese lived in the back yard, all ready to have their quills tweaked out at a minute's notice.

Before this recess stood a great arm-chair, in which the father of grandma had been laid, a new-born baby, and nearly smothered by being sat upon by the fat nurse. This thrilling fact gave it a peculiar interest to the boys; for, if great-grandpa had been smashed, where would they have been?

In front of this ancient seat stood a round table loaded with gifts, and on each side stood an Indian chief in full costume, bearing lighted Chinese lanterns on the ends of their spears, and war-clubs on their shoulders.

The arranging of these costumes had caused much labor and fun; for the splendid crowns, a foot high, were made of hen's feathers, carefully collected and sewed on to paper by Aunt Trib; the red shirts were fringed and bedecked with odd devices; leather leggings went above the warriors' knees, and all the family breast-pins were stuck about them.

Daggers, hatchets, clubs, and spears were made by the lads themselves, and red army blankets hung gracefully from their shoulders. They had planned to paint their faces blue and red, like the Feejee Islanders at Barnum's show; but Mrs. Coobiddy would not consent to have her handsome boys disfigure themselves; so the only paint they wore was nature's red in their cheeks, and heaven's blue in their eyes, as they stood by grandma's throne, smiling like a pair of very mild and happy little chiefs.

It really was a fine sight, I assure you, and grandma was quite overcome by the spectacle. So she was introduced to her gifts as quickly as possible, to divert her mind from the tender thought that all these fond and foolish adornments were to please her.

Every gift had a poem attached, and as the presents were of every description, the verses possessed an agreeable variety. Here are a few as a sample. A small tea-kettle was one gift, and this pleasing verse seemed to be bubbling out of its spout:—

"A little kettle, fat and fair,
 To sit on grandma's stove,
To simmer softly, and to sing
 A song of Freddie's love."

Another was this brief warning tucked into a match-box:—

"On this you scratch
Your little match.
When the spark flies
Look out for your eyes!
When the lucifer goes
Look out for your nose!
Little Jack gives you this
With a birthday kiss."

A third was rather sentimental, from Mrs. Coobiddy:—

"Within doth lie
A silken tie,
Your dress to deck;
 Soft and warm
 As daughter's arm
Round mother's neck."

Mr. Pib presented a mouse-trap all set; and in order to explain his poem, I must relate an incident in his varied career.

Pib had long been one of the family, and was much respected and beloved by them all. In fact, he was so petted and stuffed that he grew as fat and big as a small dog, and so clumsy that he could no longer catch the mice who dodged about among the dishes in the kitchen closets.

In vain had Mrs. Trot shut him up there; in vain had Aunt Trib told him it was his duty to clear the cupboards of such small deer. Poor fat Pib only bounced about, broke the china, rattled down the pans, to come out with empty paws, while the saucy mice squeaked scornfully, and pranced about under his very nose.

One day Trib saw Pib catch a squirrel, and having eaten it he brought the tail to her as a trophy of his skill. This displeased his mistress, and she gave him away, after a good scolding for killing squirrels and letting mice, his lawful prey, go free.

Pib was so depressed that he went into the bag without a mew or a scratch, and was borne away to his new home in another part of the town.

But he had no intention of staying; and after a

day under the sofa, passed in deep thought, and without food or drink, he made up his mind to go home. Slipping out, he travelled all night, and appeared next morning, joyfully waving his tail, and purring like a small organ.

Aunt Trib was glad to see him, and when he had explained that he really did do his best about the mice, she forgave him, and got the trap for him to give grandma, that she might no longer be annoyed by having her private stores nibbled at.

"Dear madam, with respect
My offering I bring;
The hooks all baited well,
And ready for a spring.
No more the cunning mice
Your biscuits shall abuse,
Nor put their babes to sleep
Within your fur-lined shoes.
The trap my work must do;
Forgive your portly cat,
For he, like you, has grown
For lively work too fat.
All larger, fiercer game
I gallantly defy,
And squirrel, rat and mole
Beneath my paw shall die.
So, with this solemn vow,
T. Pib his gift presents,
And sprawling at your feet
Purrs forth his compliments."

Which he actually did, and then sat bolt upright on the rug, surveying the scene with the dignity of a judge and the gravity of an owl.

Such funny presents! A wood-box and a water-carrier; a blue and gold gruel-bowl, and a black silk apron; a new diary, and a pound of remarkably choice tea; a pretty letter on birch bark, sealed with a tiny red leaf; and a bust of the wisest man in America, were some of them.

How the dear old lady did enjoy it all, and how grateful she was for the smallest trifle! An old friend sent her a lock of her mother's hair, and the sight of the little brown curl made her forget how white her own was, as she went back to the time when she last kissed that tender little mother fifty years ago.

Fearing that tears would follow the smiles too soon, Aunt Trib announced that the famous Indian chiefs, Chingchangpopocattepattle and Pockeyhockeyclutteryar, would now give a war-dance and other striking performances to represent Indian customs.

Then all sat round, and the warriors leaped into the middle of the room with a war-whoop that caused Mr. Pib to leave precipitately. It was a most exciting spectacle; for after the dance came a fight, and one chief tomahawked, scalped, and buried the other in the space of two minutes.

But the ladies mourned so for the blond little Pockeyhockeyclutteryar that he had to come alive and join in a hunting expedition, during which they shot all the chairs for buffaloes and deer, and came home to roast a sofa pillow over their fire, and feast thereupon with the relish of hungry hunters.

These exploits were brought to an end by the arrival of more friends, with more gifts, and the introduction of the birthday cake. This was cut by the queen of the *fête*, and the panting chiefs handed it round with much scuffling of big moccasins and tripping over disarranged blankets.

Then all filled their glasses with water, and drank the toast, "Grandma, God bless her!" After which the entire company took hands and danced about the big chair, singing in chorus: —

"Long may she wave, and may we all
Her dear face live to see,
As bright and well at seventy-four
As now at seventy-three."

The clock struck ten, and every one went home, leaving the family to end the day as they began it, round grandma's bed, with good-night kisses and the sound of her last words in their ears:—

"It has been a beautiful and happy day, my dears, and if I never see another you may always remember that I thought this one my best and brightest birthday."

Cambridge: Press of John Wilson & Son.

www.ingramcontent.com/pod-product-compliance
Lightning Source LLC
Chambersburg PA
CBHW060529310726
48982CB00002B/478

* 9 7 8 1 0 2 0 3 0 0 5 6 1 *